The Pink Palace:

Triple Crown Collection

The Pink Palace:

Triple Crown Collection

Marlon McCaulsky

www.urbanbooks.net

Urban Books, LLC
300 Farmingdale Road, NY-Route 109
Farmingdale, NY 11735

The Pink Palace: Triple Crown Collection

This title is published by Urban Books, LLC under a licensing agreement with Triple Crown Publications, LLC.

ISBN 13: 978-1-62286-627-4
ISBN 10: 1-62286-627-4

First Mass Market Printing January 2018
First Urban Books Trade Paperback Printing November 2015
First Trade Paperback Printing (March/April 2008)
Printed in the United States of America

10 9 8 7 6 5 4 3 2 1

This is a work of fiction. Any references or similarities to actual events, real people, living or dead, or to real locales are intended to give the novel a sense of reality. Any similarity in other names, characters, places, and incidents is entirely coincidental.

Distributed by Kensington Publishing Corp.
Submit Orders to:
Customer Service
400 Hahn Road
Westminster, MD 21157-4627
Phone: 1-800-733-3000
Fax: 1-800-659-2436

The Pink Palace:

Triple Crown Collection

Marlon McCaulsky

Dedication

This is dedicated to the memory of my brother Michael Anthony McCaulsky.

I wish I could still be with you today.
I love you.

Acknowledgments

Only God knows all the work and sacrifices made in order to get to this point. Even though I don't always do the right thing and I make mistakes, He knows my heart. So it's to Him I give all my praises.

Sheena McCaulsky, my wife, my lover, and soul mate. Without your love and support I never would have become the man I am today. Even when I was ready to give up on myself, you never stopped believing in me. Nobody has ever loved me the way you do, and I've never loved anybody the way I love you.

My hero since the day I was born, I love you, Mom (Zelpha McCaulsky). I love you, Dad (Lloyd McCaulsky). To my immediate family here and in Jamaica: I love you all very much. (It's too many of y'all to name and you know it.) My sisters, Sandra and Joanne McCaulsky, my niece Kendra McCaulsky and LeAsia, I love y'all dearly.

My family in England: Rashida Malcolm, the bond we got, cousin, can never be broken. You're like the sister I never had and always wanted. I love you. Malieka and Aqukilah couldn't have a better mum.

Charelene Malcolm, the sweetest person I have ever known. Just don't make her mad. You wouldn't like her when she's mad. I love you so much, and I'm so proud of you. God bless you, Wayne, and the kids.

My nigga Bigga, Daniel Malcolm, Evolution Entertainment at its best. Stay focused, cuz, and all your dreams will come true.

Adam Malcolm, what's up, cuz? Where you at? When you gonna come see me? Stay up, cuz.

Joan, thank you for all the little and big things you did for me when I was there. I truly appreciated the way you made me feel at home.

Mum (Mrs. B), thank you for welcoming me into your family and raising such a beautiful daughter. Thank you for believing in us from the start.

Sharon Campbell, you're the big sister I wish I had. Thank you for your support and all the advice you shared with us.

Kaisha Sherelle Campbell, thank you for loving my work. I can't believe you've grown into such a beautiful woman. You're gonna be a Top Model somewhere.

Rhianna Campbell, your feedback on my work kept me motivated to keep writing. I can't believe you've grown from a hyper little girl to a stunning young woman.

To all my other family in Birmingham, England, I love you all.

My ace from day one, Heath McKinney, we've been best friends for almost twenty years, and I can't see anybody else taking your place. Much love to you and the family.

Tito Ramos, my brother from another mother, Afro-Rican Films is gonna jump off. Much love to Yaritza and the kids. See ya soon.

Raequel A. Edgerson, a.k.a. "Roxi", my writing partner! I told you Diary Confessions is coming soon! I'm gonna give you a bottle of Bacardi for old times' sake!!

Mike Malcolm, a.k.a. Goodus, you a fool. Cuz, I've watched you grow from a crazy boy to a grown man, and I know you can do anything you put your mind to. The next time you wanna use the back seat of my car, just let me know (a.k.a. Mr. Cheap Dick LOL!) Marvin Malcolm, you gotta stay in contact with me, cuz! I know you running things down in Miami, but damn, holla at ya boy!

I love you, Janise Anderson and Tamar Humes. Don't ever forget that.

Tammy and Grenvile, we'll always be friends. I love y'all, man! Take care of my boy! Damaris DeJesus, thank you for being my friend. Ron "Double R" Gaines, stay focused and it's gonna happen for you. Shadcore, the real king of the Burg! Your day is coming. I can feel it. Swiyyah, thank you for your support, and I know it's going to happen for you too! *Don't Call Me Crazy I'm Just In Love* on sale now!! Krystal "Krys-E" Robinson, thank you for being a real friend. Now go buy my book LOL!

To my Grand Hustle Crew: Iris "Nadia" Bailey (thank you for the feedback), Tarius Bell, Shardae Bennett, Tresaca Hamilton, and Elaine Barnes, thank you for sticking by my side!

My e-mail family: Kem Cameron, loyal to the bitter end (free Mike Vick); Juanita Chemont, my book club fanatic; Karmen Moore, my fellow writer, keep on writing and it will happen!

Lewis Gilbert, Brooklyn in the house! Michael Richards, a.k.a. "Snaggle Puss" the CEO of the Royal Blue Crew LOL . . . Nikia Clarke, hey, white girl! Oh, I forgot Bohemian and Italian; Patrick Beaufort, my debate sparring partner LOL . . . I value your opinion, even if you're wrong most of the time! Tia Bethal, the voice of reason. Larissa Carter, Myca Harrison, Shamika Deck, Tanya Williams, Shenetha Daniel,

Tammy Reed (the book fiend.) You go through books like crack. I hope you enjoy this hit!

Adante Harmon, you will soon be a published author. Don't doubt your talent.

A very special thank you to, Vickie M. Stringer, for giving me a chance to be heard. You don't know how much I truly appreciate you and Triple Crown Publications for providing a company where a young author can grow. Thank you, Mia McPherson, PriScillia V. Sales, Karla Ungurean, Adam Johnson and the Triple Crown staff for all of your support. God bless you all.

A very special thank you to Cynthia Parker for your friendship and advice. We will be working together in the future, no doubt!

To everybody else that supported me over the years, thank you, too.

Prologue

Black Girl Lost

Bankhead, GA

JANELLE "MO'NIQUE" TAYLOR

I can remember the day I stopped believing in God. It's not because my father left me when I was seven and I haven't seen him since. If I did see him today I would probably spit in his face. It's not because my mother died of breast cancer when I was fourteen. As hard as that was, I guess it was her time to go. It's not even because I'm a stripper at The Pink Palace now. I got into that bullshit myself. No, the reason I stopped believing in God was because of men.

All my life men have abandoned, used, and abused me. How could God leave His world in the hands of such a simple, lustful, and disgusting creature? Because of men, there's all kinds of shit wrong in the world. If women were in charge, things would be ten times better than this crap we got now.

But don't get it twisted, shorty; this bitch ain't lesbian or bi. I can see why some women get tired of men's bullshit and go that route, but that isn't for me. I'm strictly dickly! A man has only two things going for him: his cock and his money. Half the time they can't even fuck good, always saying they'll blow ya back out and then bust too quick. Fuck that. No wonder I hustle these tricks.

It wasn't until I was sixteen that I learned the truth about how the world really works. I was still living at home on the west side of Atlanta, unaware that my life was about to pull a complete 180. I stayed near Bankhead's Techwood Projects, which had some of the city's highest crime rates. The place got demolished back in '96, forcing all its thugs to the streets. Eventually, they got a HUD house like everybody else.

Even as bad as shit was around there, I still felt safe. Before my mother died, she remarried a police officer named James. After she died, I lived with James and his sixteen-year-old son, Tony. They never supported me like my mother did. She always encouraged me to keep dancing, even going so far as to enroll me at the North Atlanta Performing High School. Although I learned most of my moves from the street, going to school helped to refine what I could already do.

By the time I was sixteen, I already had the goods to make them drool—I wore a 36C bra and my ass was round like Beyoncé's. Some of my friends said I looked like her, but I never saw it. I did, however, see the way boys looked at my body.

I had a little boyfriend back then named Shaun, and he was the only guy I had ever had sex with. As far as I could tell, he was the only guy I would ever fuck. I was crazy in love with his ass. That is, until I found out he was cheating with this chick named Wilma over in Buckhead. That was the second time a man had broken my heart. The first being my dad, of course, but I won't even talk about his lame ass.

Eventually, I got over Shaun. There were more than enough guys trying to holla at me. One boy in particular caught my eye. His name was Steven, and he was a senior at my school. Every day he would watch me dance in the performance room. He was fine as hell, too. All the girls in school were sweating him. Steven's father was a successful music producer who generously gave his son some spending cash and a new BMW to drive around. Steven had girls throwing themselves at him, but I never stooped to that level. I let him come to me.

"Hey, Janelle," Steven said to me as I walked out of the dance room one day.

"What's up, Steven?"

"You looked good in there," he said with a smile.

"I'm glad you noticed."

"I notice a lot of things."

"Yeah? Like what?"

"I notice you be alone a lot. How come?"

"I just am. Sometimes it's good to be by yourself," I remarked as Steven followed me down the hallway.

"So, do you plan on going to Skate Town Sunday night?" he asked, knowing I was there every week with my girl, Nadia.

"Maybe," I said with a smile.

"Good, I can show you some moves," he shot back confidently.

I looked him up and down.

"Whatever, just try and keep up with me." I walked slowly toward the girls' locker room, giving him one last good look at my ass before I disappeared.

***

By the time I got home that day, my stepfather, James, had already finished work and was halfway through a bottle of E&J. Since my mom's death, he had been reassigned to a desk job on the Atlanta P.D. He was forty-five years old and slightly overweight, but his six foot four inch frame hid it well. James wasn't a bad cop; he just didn't enforce every law in the book. Let's be frank—the man had a weed habit, and looking past certain drug laws allowed him to smoke in good conscience.

"Hey, James," I said as I walked by his La-Z-Boy chair. He nodded his head and looked me up and down, taking a drink of his E&J.

"Where's Tony?" he asked me.

"I don't know," I said as I walked into the kitchen. We didn't have any home-cooked meals. Most nights we ordered a pizza or had takeout. James got up from his chair, followed me into the kitchen, and stood in the doorway.

"What do you wanna eat?"

"Doesn't matter," he replied.

"Well, Chinese it is."

James just continued to look at me oddly as I dialed the number. A couple of minutes later, Tony came in and James went back to his La-Z-Boy to self-medicate.

***

Sunday night couldn't come soon enough. I was dying to see Steven at Skate Town. Of course, I couldn't let him know that. I had to stick to the script and let him come to me. To make sure that would happen, I wore some denim hot pants and a tight green top I got from Old Navy. I went to the rink with my girl, Nadia, and as soon as we hit the door, all eyes were on us.

Even though I could do without it these days, I kinda enjoyed being the center of attention back then. The looks we drew felt good, especially those from Steven, who had been staring at me from the moment I walked in. I acted like I didn't see him as I seductively moved to the desk and got a pair of skates.

Truth be told, I was better at dancing than skating, but I didn't care. As long as Steven was there, I was gonna do my thing.

"Damn, Janelle, ya boy is watching you like a hawk up in here," Nadia said to me.

"Oh, he is? Good," I replied as I put on my skates.

"He looks good, too," Nadia remarked, looking over to where Steven sat.

"Yeah, I know," I said like it was no big thing.

I started to skate around the rink, making regular eye contact with Steven. I knew what he was thinking by the way he stared at me so eagerly. It didn't take long for him to start skating behind me.

"What's up, Janelle? I see that you made it."

I turned around to skate backwards and look at him. "I'm here. I thought you were gonna show me something," I said to him.

"Oh, I'm gonna show you all my moves. It's gonna be a lot to take in." He rolled up and put his hands on my hips. I felt my panties get wet as soon as he touched me. I wanted him bad, but I couldn't fall apart just yet.

"You ain't said nothing, shorty. Talk is cheap," I said playfully.

"All right, let's do it." Steven turned me around and pulled me back, putting his crotch up to my ass. We began to dip, dive, and grind on each other as we circled the rink.

I remember thinking that if he was that good on skates, how good was he off of them? I could see the other girls looking at me with envy, but I didn't care. I had the hottest guy in the spot getting rock hard on my ass. Eat your heart out, bitches!

"Hey, Janelle, you wanna get out of here?" Steven whispered into my ear, pulling me close.

"Where we gonna go?"

"Someplace where we can just talk for a minute." I could tell by the way he held me that we wouldn't get much talking done.

"Okay."

We got our shoes and hopped into his car. He drove me to a vacant lot and parked. He pulled out a Black & Mild and opened it up, removing the tobacco filling. Then he reached in his pocket and took out a dime bag of weed. He filled the cigar paper with some broken-up chronic and rolled it up. He lit the joint and took a hit while leaning back in his seat.

"So, you ain't gonna share?" I asked him.

"Oh, my bad, shorty. I ain't know if you smoked," he said apologetically. He was lucky that he was so damn fine or I might've thought he was being stingy.

"I do occasionally," I replied as he passed me the blunt. I took me a drag. It was some really good shit. We sat in his car for a minute, puffing on the blunt and passing it back and forth. After we finished, Steven rolled another one and we puffed on that too. The radio played Usher's "U Got It Bad" as we sat in his car.

"I love this song. It's my jam," I said to him.

"Really? So who do you got it bad for?"

"Nobody," I lied. Truth was, I felt so horny for him that my panties were soaked.

"Right, I'm sure," Steven said to me cockily. I couldn't get mad at him. He had every right to be full of himself.

"Maybe you just ain't met the right one yet. Or maybe you ain't paying attention," Steven suggested as he slid his big hand up my thigh.

"Oh, I pay attention to everything. So why don't you show me what I ain't seeing?" I said.

Steven responded to my challenge by leaning over and kissing my lips. My hands wandered up his thigh and felt his dick become rock hard underneath his jeans. Steven's hand was under my shirt, fondling my soft titties. I didn't know if it was the weed or just me, but it felt like a pool was forming between my thighs. As good as my pussy was feeling, I knew I had to stop before I went over the edge.

"Steven, I gotta get home."

He pulled up off me and smiled. "All right. So when are we gonna finish what we started?"

"Real soon, I promise." It was a promise I intended to keep.

Steven drove me home, and I was as high as hell. I didn't really care, because James was probably drunk himself.

"I'll call you tomorrow," I said to Steven.

"All right." I gave him another deep kiss before I got out of his car. Damn, I was gonna fuck the shit outta him.

***

When I came in, James was up in his La-Z-Boy watching TV, drinking, and smoking a blunt. He was one hell of a father figure.

"Hey, James, what ya watching?" I asked him.

"*New Jack City.*"

"*New Jack City*? Man, I haven't seen that since I was a little girl," I said as I sat on the couch. I was still pretty worked up from being with Steven and wasn't sleepy at all.

"Where's Tony?" I asked him.

"Spending the night at his friend's house," James said as he puffed on his blunt. He looked at me then passed the weed. I was already high, so why not? I grabbed it from him and took a hit. It wasn't as strong as the weed Steven had, but it was good enough. James was definitely not gonna win father of the year, but at least I didn't have to sneak around and do stuff.

"Your mother and me used to watch this together all the time. She used to love Wesley Snipes' black ass," James said as he poured me out a glass of E&J.

"Yeah, I know. We used to watch *Jungle Fever* and the *Blade* movies together all the time," I remarked.

"You still miss her, don't you?" he asked me.

"Yeah, I do. It's just so hard to . . . to know she ain't here no more," I said to him.

James passed me the drink and I tasted it. Whoa! It was like fire in my chest. I started to cough.

"Take it slow . . . this ain't Kool-Aid. You know, the older you get, the more you look like Tina," James said to me. I took another puff of the blunt and passed it back to him.

We spent the next two hours watching *New Jack City* in silence. Somewhere between Pookie getting high and Nino Brown getting shot, I passed out.

I was so fucking high and drunk that night that I didn't remember a thing when I woke up in bed the next morning, but something didn't feel right. I was naked and under my covers, but I didn't remember getting up and going to bed. My pussy felt beat up and sore like I had been having sex all night. Then it hit me like a brick: a flash of memory that became increasingly detailed the more I thought about it. I remembered being on my back and staring at the ceiling while something heavy lay on me.

I sat up in my bed and saw my clothes on the ground. I remembered someone undressing me, but I couldn't see a face. "Oh my God . . ." I said out loud as I remembered a voice saying, *You want it, you want it*. Then I saw James' face.

I started to cry, and then I jumped up and grabbed some clothes and put them on. I ran out of my bedroom and ran into James in the hallway.

"Where do you think you're going?" he coldly said to me.

"Don't fucking touch me!" I yelled as I tried to hit him.

He grabbed my arm and pushed me up against the wall.

"You raped me! You fucking bastard!" I yelled, out of control.

"Shut the fuck up! Ain't nothing happened," he said calmly.

"You raped me! I fucking hate you!"

James put his hand over my mouth and pushed my head up against the wall. "The only thing anybody is gonna believe is that you came home drunk and high last night with that pretty boy in the BMW. There ain't no proof of me doing shit to you," he said. It took a minute for what he said to hit me. "I'm a cop, Janelle, and you're an underage girl drinking and smoking weed. Who do you think people are gonna believe?" He slowly removed his hand from my mouth.

Tears rolled down my face as I realized that he was right. Nobody would believe me.

"If you think about telling anybody about what you think happened last night . . . that would be a very bad decision," James said as he pulled his Glock from under his waist. "Now, just calm down and go back to your room."

What the hell was I gonna do then? He wasn't just a guy; he was a fucking cop, for God's sake. He could actually kill me and get away with it.

I slowly walked back to my room and closed my door. I crawled into my bed and began to sob. I felt so dirty and violated. I would have never imagined James would do anything like that to me.

I didn't go to school that day. I didn't even get out of bed. The next morning, I was still in shock about what had happened. More and more memories of what James did to me came back. He had a fucking field day, putting me in different positions and shit. Why was this happening to me? What did I do to deserve this? That was the moment I decided there was no God. I know that I wasn't no Christian, but I didn't deserve that.

I got up, got dressed for school, and walked into the kitchen. I saw Tony sitting at the table, eating a bowl of Frosted Flakes.

"You feeling better?" Tony asked me.

"What?" I responded, clueless as to what he was talking about.

"Pop said you were sick."

"He did?"

"Yeah, he said you were going through some female shit," Tony said as he took another spoonful of cereal. He had no idea what had happened. Would he have believed me if I told him? Would he believe his father, the cop, was a rapist?

Before I could say another word, James walked into the kitchen, dressed in his uniform. He stared at me coldly, making my skin crawl.

"Do y'all need a ride to school?" he asked us.

"No," I quickly said.

"Naw, I'm good, Dad. I'm riding with Lamar," Tony answered.

"Nadia is picking me up," I said.

A few minutes later, Nadia pulled up to the house and honked her horn. "I gotta go," I said, relieved to get the hell outta there.

"Be safe, Janelle," James said. His eyes told me exactly what he meant. I quickly walked out the door and to Nadia's car.

"Hey, what's up, girl?" Nadia said to me.

"Nothing. Let's go."

"Are you okay? If you're still sick, you should stay home."

"No! Can we just go?" I barked angrily.

"Damn, all right. Since when do you wanna get to school so bad?" Nadia said as she pulled off. "How did things go with Steven Sunday night?"

"Fine."

"That's it?"

"Yeah, that's it," I said sharply. I didn't wanna remember anything that happened to me that night, much less talk about it.

That whole day at school was a blur. I basically just showed up for class and said nothing. I skipped dance practice and went home and locked myself in my bedroom before James got home from work. All I could think about was how this could be happening to me. I was scared in my own home.

For the next few days, I avoided James as much as I could and locked my door at night. It was the only place I felt safe, until one night I felt somebody in the room and I woke up and saw James standing over me.

"What the hell are you doing in here? How did you get in my room?" I said, startled.

"You think I couldn't get in here anytime I wanted?"

"What do you want?" I asked him, scared to death.

"You know what I want, and you're gonna give it to me," he said to me calmly. He pulled his dick out of his pants and held it in his hands.

"I'm not doing shit with you!" I yelled.

"You thought this was over? You're the lady of the house now, and I'm the man, so it's your job to take care of me," he said as if it were a perfectly normal thing.

"You're fucking crazy!" I shouted.

James grabbed me by the back of my hair and pulled. "Listen to me, you little bitch. This is the way it is from now on. Anytime I want anything from you, it's mine. I've been taking care of you since you were eleven years old, and now it's time for you to take care of me." James shoved my face in his crotch and pushed his dick on my lips.

"Do it. Now!" he demanded.

He was going to kill me and there was nothing I could do to stop it, so I did as he said. I put it in my mouth, and James grabbed my head and shoved it down my throat. I almost choked as he violated me. I sucked his dick for about ten minutes before he pulled it out of my mouth and tucked it back in his underwear. I was numb and couldn't believe what I had just done. James smiled and walked to the door.

"That was good, Janelle, but we're gonna have to work on your technique. Your teeth scraped a little too much for me to enjoy it right," he said as he walked out of my room and closed the door.

I threw up on the floor then curled up on the ground and cried. It wasn't gonna stop. He was gonna keep on coming back and doing this to me. I had no other family to turn to. I couldn't stay there anymore, so I packed my backpack full of clothes and I left that next morning. That was the last time I was home.

I had bounced around Atlanta for eight months trying to survive the best way I could. I celebrated my seventeenth birthday in a shelter for women. I wasn't going to turn myself in to a foster care program and have them asking me questions about why I ran away from home.

Nadia's mom let me stay with her for a while without asking me too many questions. It's like they knew something was wrong but never pressured me to tell them what.

I was lucky enough to finish my junior year of high school before I dropped out. The funny thing is, James never reported me as missing, so none of my teachers asked me any questions.

I got me a little job at Taco Bell. It didn't pay much, but it kept me alive. I found my Aunt Gene's house down in Morrow and stayed with her for about six months. Aunt Gene was seventy-seven years old and living by herself. She was so happy to have the company that she never asked why a seventeen-year-old girl was moving in with her. Plus, she was a little senile, so that helped me a bit.

Like everything else in my life that had gone sour, that went wrong too. Aunt Gene's nephew down in Valdosta wanted her to move in with him and his wife. They offered to take me, but I wasn't trying to move to the country.

I was planning on moving to a little apartment and working every day at Taco Bell to pay the rent. Even doing that, I still wouldn't be able to pay any utility bills, but then the unexpected occurred.

"Come in, child! How are you?" I heard Aunt Gene say to someone at the front door. I wondered who she could have been talking to. God, I hoped she wasn't letting in another stranger or Jehovah's Witness! I went to go see who it was.

"I'm doing good, Auntie Gene. I just came by to check on you," I heard a female voice say. Who was calling her Auntie Gene? I walked into the living room and saw my cousin.

"Nikki!" I said, shocked. I hadn't seen her in like six years and she looked gorgeous. She was wearing a Dolce & Gabbana miniskirt with a matching shirt. She looked like a supermodel. Even her long black weave was on point.

"Janelle? Oh my God . . . girl, look at you!" Nikki said, surprised.

"Naw, look at you. Looking all high-fashion," I replied as she hugged me.

"Oh, I just grabbed this out of my closet. Dang, Janelle, I haven't seen you in years. You certainly filled out," Nikki remarked as she looked me up and down.

"I'm so glad you came by, darling. I've been so worried about you out in these streets," Aunt Gene said to her.

"I told you, Auntie Gene, I'm a big girl, and I'm doing fine by myself," Nikki said.

"I know, but I still worry about you."

The last I heard from Nikki, she had left home at 16 after her parents got divorced. Nikki and her mom were bumping heads so much that she had to call the police on her before she dipped. I could see that she had been doing fine. Her outfit must have cost her at least $1,000.

Aunt Gene cooked us up some fried chicken, mashed potatoes, and some collard greens. That's the one thing I loved about staying with her: I got to eat home-cooked meals again.

After dinner, Nikki gave Aunt Gene what looked like a grand in cash. We then left in her cherry red Mercedes.

"So what happened, Janelle?" Nikki asked me.

"Nothing much."

Nikki looked at me and asked again. "What happened at home, Janelle? Why are you staying with Auntie Gene here in Morrow instead of with James and Tony in Bankhead?"

It was as if she knew something bad had happened. I couldn't answer her.

"It's okay to talk to me, Janelle. Trust me, there ain't nothing you can say that would shock me," Nikki reassured me. Tears started to pool up in my eyes. Nikki pulled the car over and parked.

"It's okay, baby . . . just tell me," Nikki said as she wiped my tears. "James did something to you, didn't he?" she guessed. At that point, I completely broke down and cried.

"How did you know?" I asked her.

"Trust me, Janelle, I know the signs. I done seen it happen to so many other girls. Did he hurt you?"

I tried to hold back my tears. "I'm so stupid . . . I shouldn't have let it happen!" I yelled.

"Don't you dare blame yourself for what he did to you!" Nikki said firmly.

"You don't understand . . . I got high . . . and drunk."

"And he took advantage of you. It's okay, Janelle. We can call the cops on his ass," Nikki said.

"No!" I blurted out frantically. "You can't! He's a cop, Nikki. He'll kill me."

"Girl, he just said that to keep you from telling anybody."

"Nikki, please, I just wanna forget it happened," I begged her.

"Janelle, you cannot let him—"

"Nikki, please! Just let it go, please?"

Nikki looked at me and took a deep breath. Then she nodded her head and hugged me. She spent the next twenty minutes consoling me in the car.

Over the next few days, I started to hang out with Nikki more. She took me under her wing and bought me some new clothes. I swear she spent more money on me than anybody ever has. Gucci bags, Prada shoes, bags full of Baby Phat clothes. It made me wonder how she could she afford all that. She didn't exactly go to work every day and punch a clock.

We were eating lunch at California Pizza Kitchen in Lenox Mall when I decided to ask her. "Nikki, thank you. I mean, nobody has ever treated me like this."

"Janelle, you're family, and you deserve to be spoiled after what you went through," Nikki replied.

"But you've been spending a lot of money."

"Girl, money ain't a thing."

"How come?" I asked.

Nikki looked at me, and then took another mouthful of her Jamaican Jerk chicken pizza.

"Nikki, come on. I know you don't got a regular job. You said you were in the entertainment field, but I know there's more to it."

"I told Auntie Gene the entertainment field 'cause she wouldn't understand. I'm a dancer, Janelle."

"You mean a stripper," I said bluntly.

Nikki smiled. "That's right. I make more money in one night than most people make in a month."

"Damn, you don't even look like a stripper. How long have you been doing it?"

"For a month now. Janelle, I'm gonna be real with you. Auntie Gene is moving to Valdosta. You working at Taco Bell ain't gonna cut it, so what's your game plan?"

"I'm just gonna do what I gotta do."

"Janelle, I ain't trying to hate on you, but I gotta be honest. You're a high school dropout working at Taco Bell. How long do you think you're gonna last out here?"

I didn't know what to say at that point.

"Look, Janelle, you look fucking sexy as hell, and you can dance your ass off. You can make some serious money."

I had to admit, Nikki was making a whole lot of sense. I did need to make some money.

"All I have to do is dance?"

"If that's all you wanna do. Listen, these niggas in the clubs ain't nothing but some tricks. They might wanna call you a bitch or a ho, but they spend they whole paycheck on you and get nothing but a hard-on at the end of the night. The only time I mess with any nigga is when he's ballin'. All the money I spent on you this weekend? I'm gonna make it all back tonight," Nikki said.

"All right, I don't care what I have to do. I need some money."

Later that night Nikki took me to The Pink Palace in midtown Atlanta. I saw why they called it The Pink Palace. Other than the huge, pink neon sign outside, it had plush, pink leather couches and chrome interiors that made me felt like I was in a music video. This was not the kind of place I had envisioned a strip club to be. The place was packed with ballers and shot callers and girls that looked like models.

I watched as the dancers did their thing on stage. Most of them popped, jiggled, and rolled as niggas emptied they pockets. If that's all it took, I knew I could make a lot of money up in there. The DJ was bumpin' and Hpnotiq was flowing.

When Nikki got on stage in her baby-doll lingerie, the men went crazy! She swung around the stage's chrome pole like an Olympic athlete, slowly undressing herself. Niggas were pushing twenties and fifties in between her pink G-string. She was hustling these niggas like a pro! If she could do this, so could I.

After Nikki's routine ended, she came and took me backstage. She took out her money and counted it. She had made $380 from one dance.

"So, what do you think? You ready to make this money?" Nikki asked me.

"Yeah, I'm down to get this money, fo'sho."

"So, what's your stage name gonna be?"

I thought about it for a second and then it came to me. "Mo'Nique, my middle name," I told her.

"Sounds good. Just remember every nigga in here is a trick. Don't let yourself get caught up. Only tricks with cash can get some ass. You feel me?" Nikki said to me seriously.

"Yeah, I do."

***

The next day, I moved in with Nikki and her homegirl, Penny, who was a dancer at The Pink Palace They lived in a four-bedroom house in Morrow. Penny was nice. She was the only girl Nikki was really cool with at the club. For the first time in a long time I felt at home.

My first night dancing at the club my heart was racing out of control. Nikki gave me a glass of vodka to calm me down. All the other girls stared at me and whispered things to each other. I knew I intimidated them with my looks. I had on a sheer black thong and lace bra that Nikki had bought me from Victoria's Secret.

"How do you feel?" Nikki asked.

"Nervous as hell."

"Don't be. Just go out there and do your thing. You'll be fine."

The DJ started to play R. Kelly's "Feelin' on Yo Booty" as I slowly walked on stage. *I can do this shit*, I thought to myself. I was a better dancer than any of the girls in there. I had never been naked in front of a room filled with horny-ass men, but there was no turning back now.

I slowly started to grind my waist to the beat, making eye contact with as many men as possible. I could tell that they were in awe of my body. Some men stared with their mouths open.

I dipped down low at the edge of the stage and parted my thighs, giving this one guy a closer view of the fat pussy lips peeking through my thong. He touched me softly and pushed a twenty between my panty straps.

I tried to remember how Nikki had worked the stage the other night, and I did the same thing. I turned around and unclasped my bra, letting it drop to the floor while I covered my breasts with my other hand. I seductively revealed myself to the horny crowd as they threw tens, twenties, and fifties onstage. I rubbed my tits and allowed another guy to fondle them as he gave me a hundred dollar bill. I was on my hands and knees, still grinding to the song as I crawled the stage like a black panther. This was a dance I used to do in school, but never half-naked.

I slithered my thong off of me and rolled my ass in one guy's face, making my pussy pop. He was mesmerized by my ass and muttered something that I couldn't hear. I lay on my back, spread my legs, and gyrated my waist, simulating an orgasm as he slipped a fifty into my garter. I think he came on himself as he breathed heavily through his mouth. When the song ended, I made sure to pick up every dollar that was on stage.

When I got behind the curtain, I quickly counted up my earnings, and to my surprise, I had over $500 in my hands. Becoming a dancer was definitely the right move to make.

"Damn, girl, you were better than I thought you would be! You had them tricks hypnotized for real. So, how do you feel, Mo'Nique?" Nikki asked me.

"Like I just got some money from the ATM!" I exclaimed.

"Trust me, Mo, this ain't nothing compared to what we're gonna be making."

1

I'm a Hustler

College Park, GA
Two years later

JAYSON HARPER a.k.a. TOMMY HOLLOWAY

"You know, Tommy, outta all these niggas here, you're the only one I really trust," Damien says to me. I don't know why, but I'm always surprised when I hear somebody say that. Here we are, surrounded by dudes that he's been down with for years, and I've only known Damien for four months.

"Yeah, dawg, you know I'm gonna hold you down," I say back to him as I give him some dap. Damien takes his .45 automatic, tucks it in his pants, and pulls down his Pelle Pelle shirt.

We walk out to the black Navigator parked outside. This has become something like a routine every Tuesday afternoon—we ride out to the trap house and collect that week's profit. Nothing has ever gone wrong, but you can never be too careful.

Damien is the kind of cat who's ready for anything at any time—a real live nigga. I'm the same way, too, but unfortunately for him, I'm only playing the role of Tommy Holloway, a hustler from Chicago. I've been in deep cover, infiltrating College Park's drug dealing circuit.

For the past year, a major crew from New York has been locking down the area. They call themselves the Flip Set outta Harlem. The main man, a big time hustler named Dwayne "King" Smith, calls all the shots from up north. As King's right hand man, Damien Ruffin was sent down here to set up shop.

Most of the local hustlers don't want to deal with the heat King and the Flip Set bring, so they set up shop elsewhere, but there are some local hustlers who don't mind going to war over a spot they've worked hard to build up. Dre is one of those local, corner hustlers who isn't going to roll over easy.

As we pull up to the trap, I spot a car of his boys following us. I know what time it is.

"Yo, Damien, check it out," I say as I stop at a light.

"What is it?"

"Right there on the corner." I gesture toward the car.

"Oh, so them niggas wanna do it like that?" Damien says as he pulls out his .45. Damien is the type of nigga to shoot up the whole hood and not give a damn, so I act first and bend the corner, peeling out in front of them. I pull out my nine and bust three shoots at the hood of the car.

"Yo! What you doing, Tommy?" Damien yells.

"Keeping us alive."

Dre's boys bust a few shots back at us and pull off in the opposite direction.

"Fuck them niggas! Turn around!" Damien yells.

"Nigga, we can't have a shootout in front of the spot. We gonna have cops all over the place!"

Damien looks at me and nods his head. "You're right. Good looking out."

Besides, having a gun fight in a neighborhood filled with kids playing outside isn't what I wanna see happen. By me shooting first and getting us outta an ugly position only proves to Damien how down I really am. Lying and manipulating different situations is what I've always been good at.

It's probably one of the reasons Lauren left me. Can't say I blame her. Our marriage was doomed from the beginning. I'm surprised it lasted as long as it did with me being a cop. Marrying a woman because she reminds you of your ex-girlfriend is always a sure promise that it will end in divorce.

After things get funky up in College Park, I break out and drive up to the spot in Decatur, where I meet with my contact, Lt. McNiven. McNiven is the one that hand-picked me from my department in Savannah.

"Lieutenant," I acknowledge him by his title.

"Harper. So what happened today?" McNiven asks.

"Dre's boys rolled up on us on our way to the spot, but I was able to get us out of there before things got messy."

"Dre is getting tired of sharing the streets with Damien. I think we should probably bring them in and stop this from becoming an all-out war."

"No, I got it under control. Lieutenant, if you bring Damien in now, everything we've worked so hard for just to get close to King goes out the window," I say as McNiven turns and paces back and forth. "Lieutenant, King is the key . . . and I'm this close to him. Now's not the time."

McNiven paces some more. "Okay, but if bodies start popping up, I'm pulling you out and I'm shutting them down."

"Understood," I answer.

"All right, be careful, Jayson," McNiven says to me.

"I always am."

Later that night, I drive over to the spot and meet up with Damien. We roll out to The Pink Palace, a local strip club where he's fucking a dancer named Nikki. She wants to introduce me to her cousin, Mo'Nique.

"Yo, Tommy, when you see Nikki's cousin, I swear you gonna flip," Damien says.

"Yeah, right. She'd better not be a buttaface."

"Man, you've seen Nikki. What do you think her cousin gonna look like?"

"I don't know," I say hesitantly.

"Nigga, you lucky I'm hooking you up like this. As fine as Mo'Nique's is, I would be hittin' that shit, too, if it weren't for Nikki tripping every time I'm around her."

"Nikki ain't stupid, nigga. She knows your ass!" I say as Damien starts to laugh.

"Damn right," Damien proudly remarks as he gets out of his truck.

When we walk into The Pink Palace, we sit at Damien's regular table, ordering a bottle of Moët and sparking up a blunt. The Palace is filled with the usual horny pimps and playas. The women in The Palace are straight up Booty Talk material. I swear they have asses that come in all shapes and sizes. The DJ drops "Like a Pimp," and the girls on stage start to work their asses to the beat.

Then the main lights in the club get dim, and a spotlight shines on center stage. The curtain opens, and a girl steps out. Every man's dick in the club gives her a standing salute.

"That's Nikki's cousin, Mo'Nique. What you got to say now, nigga?" Damien braggingly says.

I gotta give it up to Damien on this one, Mo'Nique is a dime for real. Shit! She got every man ogling and nuttin' up in their pants and she knows it. Mo'Nique's a thick sister. She's about 5 feet 5 inches tall with long, jet-black hair, skin the color of brown caramel, and some sexy-ass lips. She has a flat stomach and a slim waistline that makes her ass look even bigger and rounder than it already is, and a tattoo on her lower back that says "Mo' Betta." Couldn't be more right.

It's hypnotizing the way she moves her body like a belly dancer. Her light brown eyes are seductive. She bends over and touches her toes, making her ass clap. She looks over at our table and sees Damien and me sitting there. I guess Nikki told her about me and she sees dollar signs. She walks off the stage and over to me and begins to pop her pussy. I ain't gonna lie; she has my dick harder than a brick.

"I told you I was gonna take care of you, nigga," Damien says to me.

I can't bother to answer him because Mo'Nique straddles me and starts to nibble on my ear. Her sheer black thong rubs on my pants, and my dick is screaming to be let loose. Then she eases up and walks back on stage and disappears back behind the curtain.

"So, what you gonna do with all that ass, son?" Damien asks.

"I'll figure something out."

DAMIEN RUFFIN

It's a good thing I found a loyal nigga like Tommy to roll with down here. This nigga got heart. I like that. The funny thing is, at first I didn't trust him. Some slick-talking nigga from Chicago hustling down south in the same spot we were in? I thought he was five-o for sure, but he proved himself to me and saved my life.

We were picking up a delivery from King three months ago with Corey, Quan, and Horse, when Dre and his niggas tried to jack us. Tommy pulled out and blasted a nigga getting ready to pop me. Even though Corey's dumb ass doesn't like him, I still got love for that nigga. Tommy's more reliable than his dumb ass anyway.

That's why I put him up on Nikki's fine-ass cousin, Mo'Nique. Shit! I wanna fuck her ass myself! Not that Nikki ain't fine, but damn, Mo got a fat ass! I don't know what it is about these Southern girls, but they all seem to be thick as shit. Nikki is my main bitch down here. Sure, I trick around, but Nikki is my personal Foxy Brown.

Fuck Dre's country ass. Do they even know who they fucking with? If this was Harlem, I would have one of my little shorties bodybag this mutherfucka! King told me to be careful fucking with these down south niggas. He said just because these niggas have a Southern drawl, don't think them niggas are slow.

Atlanta is definitely a different world than Harlem. People love it here. Must be the weather. All this Southern hospitality was weird to me at first. In New York we don't say shit to somebody we don't know if we walking by them. Mind your own business is the rule of thumb when walking the streets.

Nikki certainly used that Southern charm on me when I first met her in The Pink Palace. Not that she had to try hard to get my attention. She was the finest thing in the club that night. Soon as she heard a nigga's accent and saw me flossin' up in there, she knew I was that nigga to be with.

"What up, ma?" I say to Nikki.

"Nothing, baby. I was just waiting for you to get here," Nikki says.

"Bring your fine ass here."

Nikki walks over to me, and I grab two hands full of that fat ass. Nikki looks at Tommy.

"So, Tommy, do you like my cousin?" she asks him.

"Hell, yeah. Where is she?"

"She's getting changed. She'll be out in a minute."

"Good. Get your stuff. We gonna bounce back to the crib," I say.

"Is something bothering you, baby?" she asks.

"Naw, just hurry up. I'll be out front." I walk out to the truck and roll up another blunt. That shit today with Dre's boys is still fucking with me. I never used to let any nigga like that try me. Tommy keeps saying that when the time's righ,t we'll smash on dem niggas. I trust his judgment for now, but sooner or later this nigga is gonna get dealt with.

Nikki walks outside and gets in the truck with me. I don't say anything to her, but honey knows what to do to relax a nigga when I'm tense like this. She slides her hand up my thigh and feels on my dick.

"What ya doing, ma?"

"I'm just playing with my big man." She unzips my pants, pulls out my dick, and slips the head into her mouth. She slowly slobs me down with a whole lot of saliva, just the way I like it.

"Oh, shit . . ." Shorty was definitely a head doctor. "Damn, ma . . . what about your cousin and Tommy?"

She doesn't even slow down and continues to suck the skin off my dick. About five minutes later, I bust a nut in her mouth, and she slurps it down.

"Oh God . . ." I utter in total bliss.

"There. Didn't that make you feel better?"

"Hell yeah." That's why she's my main bitch. She knows how to take care of her nigga. I don't even mind trickin' on her. Any girl who can suck a mean dick like that deserves it.

I put the truck in drive, get on I-85 South, and head to my spot down in College Park. I love staying in this part of town. It's near the airport and just outside of Atlanta. Plus, the crack heads are like the *Night of the Living Dead* here. They never go to sleep!

Nikki certainly puts my mind at ease with that good brain she gives. I can't wait to get her ass in my crib so I can break that back.

We pull up to my place about fifteen minutes later.

"You sure got here quickly," Nikki says to me.

"Well, you gave me all the motivation I needed, ma."

"Did I? So you ready for the main event, daddy?" Nikki coos in that sexy-ass voice as she moves her hand up her thick brown thighs and pulls her skirt up for me.

"You damn right."

We walk into the house and I toss my keys on the coffee table, grabbing Nikki by the waist and unzipping her miniskirt. I pull her G-string down, take out my still hard dick, and rub the head up and down her wet slit. Fuck using a condom. I wanna feel all that gushy pussy on my dick, and she wanna feel it too.

"Ummmm . . . put it in, daddy," Nikki moans out.

I give her what she wants as I push my dick inside her wet walls. I lift her leg and give her some long, deep strokes. I swear she gets wetter than a waterfall when I'm inside her. I love how she clenches on to my dick with her fat lips when I go up in her.

"Oh, shit! Fuck me, daddy! Give me that good dick!" Nikki exclaims.

"Oh, you like that nasty shit?" I ask her as I smack her ass.

"Yeah . . . I . . . love it! Give it to me!"

I pick her up and continue to give her the business as I carry her to the couch and lay her down. I push her legs back and stare at that juicy pussy. Damn, I swear I ain't never had a freak like her before and I've fucked plenty of bitches.

"Put it back in, daddy . . . Ahhhh," she moans as I stab that fat pussy. I get up on that ass and start to bang her like a jackhammer while she moans at the top of her lungs. Damn, her shit feels so good! She'll make a nigga come quick if I ain't careful.

For the rest of the night, I'm fucking the shit outta Nikki. I swear she got more stamina than I do. I know she done cum at least three times already and she still wet. I hope Tommy is hitting Mo'Nique's fat ass tonight. If he don't, then I'm gonna tap that shit sooner or later.

MO'NIQUE

I'm a hustler, and these fools throwing money at me are my customers. They more like dope fiends who can't get enough of my shit. The most these dumb winos get is just a peek of my precious pussy. They're lucky if they even get a whiff of my sweet juices. Only a few select clientele get to feel my goodies.

Nikki puts me on to some big-time hustlers from New York she's messing with. She's had this dude Damien trickin' on her for the past five months or so. She says she wants to hook me up with his friend, Tommy. Normally, I don't fuck with the broke-ass niggas that roll up in here, but hustlers with huge bank accounts are the exception to the rule.

When I see Tommy with Damien, he don't look like what I thought he would. He is tall, with a tight bald fade and a freshly shaven goatee. He wears a spotless button-down shirt, a nice, diamond-encrusted cross around his neck, and all-white Air Force Ones. Shit, this dude is fine. But he's still a trick.

I come out and see him sitting at the table drinking. "So, you must be Tommy," I say as I sit at his table.

"And you must be Mo'Nique. Thank you for the dance."

"Just doing my job. So, Tommy, you from around here?"

"Naw, I'm from Chi-Town. I'm just down here on business." Tommy takes another sip and glances up at me.

"Yeah, Nikki said you and Damien were partners."

"Something like dat. So, where you from, Mo'Nique?"

"Bankhead."

"Do you wanna drink?" he asks me.

"Sure." He pours me out a glass of Moët.

I don't know what it is, but there's something different about this guy. When I met Damien the first time, I knew what that nigga was all about. He's been trying to get at me behind Nikki's back for a while now.

I look into Tommy's eyes and try to get a feel for him. He smiles and takes a drink.

"So, do you wanna get outta here?" he suggests.

"You don't like the view?" I playfully ask.

"I do. I'd just rather view it in private."

I got no doubt where this is heading and what he wants. As sexy as he is, that's all he has to say.

"Okay, but there is a price for a private viewing."

Tommy pulls out a money clip and peels out $1,200. "Am I covered?" he asks.

"No doubt."

We slip out of the club and walk to his Cadillac XLR-V. The butter-soft interior hugs my body as I melt into the seats. Tommy gets in and turns the key, making the engine turn over. He shifts the stick into reverse and backs out of the parking lot.

Changing gears again, he speeds off down the street, handling the car nicely as he dips from lane to lane on I-85 South. He's quiet most of the ride, as if he's lost in thought, a thousand miles away. Most of the niggas I deal with are too busy telling me this or that, bragging about what a baller they are, but Tommy is so low-key. It's like he has the quiet confidence of a stone-cold hustler that doesn't need to prove anything to anybody.

We exit off on 69 and on to Old National Highway. We soon turn down a street and enter an apartment complex, pulling up to a town-house.

"This is way back in the cut," I say to Tommy.

"Yeah, it's nice and quiet back here."

We walk to the front, and Tommy shuffles for his keys and opens the door. He flips on the lights and we walk in. I look at his nicely deco-rated place.

"Nice place," I say as I walk around his big liv-ing room.

"Thanks. Make yourself at home."

This guy is definitely different from the other tricks I mess with. Most guys are trying to fuck me on the doorsteps by the time we get to their crib.

"Do you wanna drink?"

"No, I'm fine." I decide to find out a little bit more about this guy. "So, where's wifey?" I teasingly ask.

"She left me a long time ago," he responds.

I wasn't really expecting him to give me a real answer to that. He walks into the kitchen, and I walk into his bedroom. This guy is not flashy at all. His bedroom is simple and clean. He has a neatly made king-size bed, a flat screen, forty-nine-inch TV hanging on the wall, and a black dresser. Even though I know this guy is a hustler, he certainly doesn't live like it.

Then I feel him gently kiss my neck and caress my breasts. I close my eyes and feel my floodgates open, releasing my sexual juices. I can't believe I'm feeling this turned on.

I turn around and undress myself for him. He begins to help me pull off my top. I unzip his pants and find his hard dick. I'm about to give him some head when he stops me. Instead, he gently pushes me back on the bed, pulls off my thong, and softly kisses my stomach all the way up to my breasts, tracing his tongue around my areolas and sucking on my nipples.

This is the first guy to give me foreplay. He teasingly kisses my neck as he lies between my legs, rubbing up against my privates. My legs wrap around his waist, pulling him closer, rubbing his dick between my pussy lips. I've never yearned so much to feel a man inside of me.

Tommy slips on a condom. His dick parts my fat pussy lips and rubs my clitoris, then he slides inside of me.

"Ahhhh," I moan as his rock hard dick deeply penetrates. I lift my head, look down, and watch his thick member push in and out of me. It turns me on even more.

"Yessss . . ." I shamelessly moan.

Deeper and deeper he drives his dick as I cum again and again. We change positions, with me on top, then we roll over while continuing to passionately sex each other. He lifts my leg and rests it on his shoulder as he digs deeper inside me.

His stamina is incredible. Most guys would bust a nut within 10 minutes of being inside my juicy walls, but Tommy stays hard, stroking me. Tommy isn't a selfish lover like most guys trying to catch a nut. He seems more interested in making sure I am pleased.

I hate to admit it, but I find myself enjoying the sex even more than he seems to be. I'm beginning to think of this as more of a date than me freaking a trick.

Tommy pulls out of me, and I turn and bend over for him. He enters me doggie-style. My wetness allows him to slide right back in me with ease. I feel his dick grow bigger inside me. I've never been with dick so good. He hits it so deep from the back that I can feel it in my chest. Each stroke in me goes farther, as I enjoy the feeling of his balls slapping against my ass cheeks.

"Oh, shit!" I yell out as I climax, cumming harder than ever before.

Tommy keeps on stroking my now-hypersensitive clit as his own orgasm is approaching. I close my eyes and feel like a trapped love slave, unable to move and forced to enjoy this unmanageable sensation that runs through my pussy and down my legs. Then, finally, I feel his penis head swell with a powerful surge of cum into the condom. Tommy collapses on my back, completely drained, enjoying his orgasm.

I fall asleep and wake up in the morning. Damn, I can't believe I did that. Most of the time after we're done cutting, I get my shit together and bounce outta there, but this time I felt so relaxed and drained I couldn't even move.

Tommy is already up and dressed. I walk into the kitchen, wrapped in the bed sheet. He has already made me some eggs and toast.

"Are you hungry?" he asks me.

"Yeah." I sit at the table and we eat our breakfast quietly. This is too weird. Why does he treat me like this and why do I want to see him again?

"Is there somewhere I can drop you off?" he asks.

"Yeah, I'll get dressed."

"Maybe we can see each other again?"

Why do I feel so happy to hear him say that? "Yeah, I think that will be all right."

2

Play Your Position

JAYSON

I meet up with Quan and Corey at the trap to see if Dre and his boys are still rolling around clockin' us. Damien brought them down from New York to set up shop with King's nigga, Horse.

Quan is nineteen, a smart dude that gets shit done. Not just street smart but school smart, too. Every time I see him he's got his nose in a book. I think he's reading *The Da Vinci Code* again. We debate different topics all the time. Honestly, it makes no sense for him to be hustling with these career thugs.

Corey, on the other hand, is a dumb ass. He's twenty and hotheaded. King wanted to get Corey out of his hair, so he sent him down to Atlanta with Damien. He's the type of nigga you can't tell nothing to, 'cause he thinks he knows it all when he really don't know shit. This cat thinks he's the new Nino Brown of the hood or some shit. If the Flip Set has a weakness, it's this nigga. He's always trying to prove himself to Damien, but the truth is, Damien is more impressed with Quan, because he knows how to play his position.

Horse is the muscle of the group, an old hood nigga King was locked up with back in '96. Horse began serving jail time in '91 for robbing a grocery store up in Yonkers. The two became friends at Rikers. King promised Horse that if he watched his back inside, he would set him up with both some paper and a position in his set when he got out. When Horse was released in 2005, King kept his word. Horse is down to ride on anybody and got no problem getting locked up again.

"Yo, Quan, what it do?" I ask him.

"Same old shit, man," Quan replies. "The fiends keep on coming back for more."

"So in other words, business is good."

"Yeah, I guess." Quan picks up his book and continues to read.

Just then Corey walks by, acting hard.

"What up, nigga?" Corey says to me, dressed in a wifebeater and baggy jeans. He keeps his strap in his waist at all times. Sometimes I think he's going to fuck around and shoot his dick off.

"What up?" I say to him.

"Nothing, nigga. . . . You reading another book, nigga?" Corey says to Quan.

"Yeah, so?" Quan replies.

"Man, you think a fucking book is gonna teach you something? Fuck a book! You need to watch how I do this shit. Get this money," Corey says to him.

"Maybe if you picked up a book every now and then you might learn something."

"No thick, dusty-ass book gonna teach me shit, son. You need to get your paper up," Corey says.

Quan shakes his head.

"And you need to stop being so damn ignorant, nigga," I say.

"Whatever, man." Corey walks to the door. A fiend comes up to the house and Corey sells him two rocks of crack for ten dollars.

"Let me ask you something, Q, if you don't mind," I say to Quan.

"Naw, man, go ahead."

"What are you doing here, man?" I ask.

"What do you mean?" he says as I sit down on the couch.

"I mean, I see why Corey hustles. He's a fucking dumbass. But you, you should be in college doing something with your life."

"Well, you know . . . sometimes shit happens. Where I'm from, you either sell rock or get shot. College isn't much of an option. Besides, I got my mom and little sister up in Marcy Projects that I gotta take care of. I can't do that in college."

I guess even the smart kids fall through the cracks.

For the past couple of days, I've been thinking about Mo'Nique. I guess I've been trying to get over this divorce shit for the past year and a half. I haven't been dating anybody. A woman can't deal with the shit that goes down in my line of work.

I can tell Mo'Nique is surprised I'm treating her like a woman instead of a ho. Maybe I should, seeing that I'm undercover. I should stay in character, but a girl that fine shouldn't be swinging around poles all night. She's not a genuine gold digger like her cousin, Nikki—not yet, anyway. Even though she's a stripper, I can see a bit of innocence in her eyes. She could make a good wife someday. Not that I'm a good man who deserves a good wife. I already fucked up my own marriage.

Mo'Nique's fine ass is just the thing I need to put Lauren out of my mind. Mo'Nique's using me to come up, and I'm using her to get off. Damn, the sex is good, and honey got a body on her to kill for: butter-soft skin, long, thick legs, and a pussy a man could drown in. Must be why I've been thinking about her since the other day.

I pick up my cell and call her number.

"Hello?" Mo'Nique answers.

"Mo'Nique?"

"Yeah . . . Tommy?" she asks.

"Yeah, what's up?"

"Nothing, I'm just at the house, chilling. What are you doing?"

"Nothing, just thinking about you. Do you wanna do something?" I ask her.

She pauses for a moment. "Yeah, that's cool."

"All right, I'll be at your place in 10 minutes," I say as I turn onto 75 South.

"Okay."

I hang up and head to her house. She's staying in Morrow with Nikki, another dancer called Penny, and Penny's baby. When I pull up to the house, I notice the ghetto-ass hood they stay in. Some kids playing outside stop and stare at my car as I get out with my $200 Oakleys on.

I knock and Penny opens the door.

"You must be here to see Mo," Penny says to me. She's dressed in a bikini top that can barely hold her luscious D-cup titties, and some hot pants that expose her fat ass.

"Yeah."

"Come in."

As I walk in, I see clothes and baby bottles on the living room floor. It's as if the floor is one big laundry basket.

"Her room's down the hall."

"Thanks."

Penny eyes me up and down and presses her big-ass titties on my chest as I walk by her down the narrow hallway.

I knock on Mo'Nique's door. She opens it up, and it's like night and day. Her room is spotless and tidy. She's dressed in a red fitted T-shirt that stops just above her belly button, showing off the tattoo on her lower back. She's got on some Baby Phat jeans that conform to her incredible ass.

"Hey," she says.

"Hey, girl, you ready?"

"Yeah, let's go."

We walk out of the house and get in my car.

"Where are we going?" she asks me.

"You hungry?"

"Yeah, a little," she says with a smile.

I smile back at her. Damn, there's something about her pretty brown eyes. I can't help but stare, and she knows I can't help it. She blushes.

"Why do you look at me like that?" she asks me.

"Because it don't take a whole day to recognize sunshine," I reply.

She smiles and shakes her head. Man, I just wanna kiss her soft body again.

I pull off and drive to Southlake Mall. We walk inside, and it's packed with black people walking and talking to each other. A group of brothers seated at a nearby table stare and point at Mo'Nique as we walk by. She is the type of girl that demands attention. We go to the Japanese restaurant in the food court, and I order some rice and teriyaki chicken for us. We sit at a table and eat.

"Do you always go out with men you meet at the club?"

She looks up at me as if deciding whether or not she should answer the question. "No, not always, but I guess I did sleep with you that night. I can see why you would think that."

"I didn't ask you that to insult you. I just wanna know if you really wanna be with me or if Damien put you up to it."

"He didn't. Nikki told me about you and said that you were cute. If I didn't think so, I wouldn't have left with you."

"Oh."

A moment of awkward silence goes by. "So, why did your wife leave you?"

Now I decide whether I should tell her the truth or not.

"She didn't like my day job," I answer, keeping my response short and purposely vague.

"I don't like my night job either," she says.

"Then why do you do it?" I ask her.

"Because it pays better than working at Taco Bell."

I chuckle and so does she. We continue to eat. The three brothers sitting at the table get up and walk over to us. They stop and stand behind Mo'Nique.

"I knew I knew that tattoo from somewhere. You be freak dancing at The Pink Palace, don't ya?"

Mo'Nique turns around and looks at them. "So? Who the fuck are you?" she snaps back.

"Whoa, don't trip. My niggas just wanted to know could you work a little something right here for us? We got plenty of singles," he says as they laugh.

Mo'Nique stares at them, humiliated and not knowing what to say, so I cut in.

"She's off the clock, but I'll be happy to take your money."

"Oh, sorry, partner. I ain't mean to be rude, but you got a real freak here. You a real lucky man. Bend over to the front and touch ya toes!" he sings.

"What you say, nigga?" I growl as I get up from my chair. His two punk-ass friends look me up and down.

"Tommy, it's all right. Let's just go," Mo'Nique says, sensing my anger.

"Yeah, Tommy, this ain't the time to play Captain-Save-a-Ho." They laugh again.

I chuckle and look at Mo'Nique then grab the punk by his shirt, slamming his head down on the table. He doesn't know what hits him. His boys start to come at me, and I raise my shirt and show them my heat.

"You don't want none of that, do you?" They both back off. "Now, say you're sorry, bitch."

"Tommy, let him go," Mo'Nique says, looking around to see if mall security is coming.

"As soon as I hear what I'm waiting for." I push his face into my food.

"Sorry! I'm sorry! I'm sorry!" he pleads. I let him go and his face is covered with rice and sauce.

"Let's go," I say to Mo'Nique. "Y'all be good, boys." We walk out of the mall.

"I'm sorry that happened," Mo'Nique utters after we're in the parking lot.

"You don't have to apologize. You didn't do anything."

"That's why I hate my job," she says in a regretful tone.

"Maybe you should start looking in the *AJC* classifieds," I joke.

She smiles and we get in my car.

MO'NIQUE

As we drive down the street, I can't help but think about what Tommy did for me in the mall. No man has ever stood up for me like that. Did he lose his cool because he felt like they were dissin' him for being with a stripper or because he genuinely cares for me? *Stop that,* I tell myself. *He's not trying to turn a ho like me into a housewife. I just gotta stay focused and remember that he's just another trick. This is business.*

We head back to his place. The area looks more familiar in the daytime than it did the other night. I used to drive through College Park with Nikki when she was messing with Dre two years ago. Some of his homeboys were trying to holla at me, but I wasn't trying to mess with a nigga who was a do-boy for another nigga. Besides, that was Nikki's hustle.

Dre used to give her fat rolls of cash, and we would go to the mall and buy all kinds of Gucci bags and Versace dresses. She had Dre's nose wide open. Nikki was a pro, and I was just soaking up the game from her. Even at The Pink

Palace she would tell me not to fuck around with those small-time hustlers, that if I was going to give a nigga some ass, make sure he was ballin' with mad cash.

We get to Tommy's place, and I sit out on the balcony, admiring the view. Tommy comes outside and sits next to me and gives me a Coke.

"So, how did you start dancing?" he asks me.

"Nikki put me on."

"Oh. It just surprises me when I see a girl as beautiful as you stripping for a living," he says.

"You don't know how many times I've heard a man say that to me. I guess I'm just waiting for something better to come along."

"Why wait? Why don't you find something else?" he asks.

Once again he surprises me. Most tricks tell me that they can take care of me and all I have to do is be by their side.

"I don't know."

"Why not go to college? There are plenty of schools in Atlanta."

"You sure you ain't Captain-Save-a-Ho?" I ask him.

"Naw, I was just asking."

I didn't have to say that to him. It was just a question.

"Well, I never graduated from high school, so college was out," I admit.

"What happened?"

I look out at the view from the balcony and tell him the truth. "When I was twelve, my mom got remarried to a cop named James, but then two years later she passed away from breast cancer. So it was just James, his sixteen-year-old son, Tony, and me. James wasn't exactly the best parent. Tony and me pretty much came and went as we pleased. James was hurt really bad by my mom's death and drowned himself in E&J and weed. He used to let us drink and smoke with him in the house.

"This one night, I got so high I couldn't even get up off the couch. I guess James carried me to my room and put me in bed. He then started to undress me. I was so blown I could barely move. By the time I knew where I was, James already took off my bra and panties and was groping me and shit. The next thing I felt was him ramming his dick in between my legs. All I could do was lie there and let him do what he wanted to me.

"After he was done, he got a towel and cleaned me up and took a shower. Then he told me nobody would believe the word of a high and drunk sixteen-year-old girl over a respected cop. Muthafucka . . . I was so scared and ashamed that I believed him.

"I ran away a week later and dropped outta school. For about two years, I bounced around Atlanta and crashed at different friends' houses. Then I met up with Nikki at my aunt's house and she took me in."

I don't know why I told him all that. I've never told anybody, except Nikki, about what happened to me. Tommy didn't say anything. He just took my hand and stood up and walked me to the bedroom. I guess he didn't bring me here to play Dr. Phil. Nikki said that in this game, nobody is gonna feel sorry for you, so don't expect to get sympathy. Tommy just wants to fuck me, and I just want his cash, so let's just get to it.

To my surprise, Tommy lays me on the bed, spoons up behind me, and just holds me. It isn't sexual at all. I just feel so safe and warm in his arms. I haven't felt this way since . . . my mom was alive. I'm supposed to dance at The Palace tonight, but I end up falling asleep in his arms.

When I wake up, it's four in the morning and Tommy's still holding me, half-asleep. I feel his dick grow harder as it rubs up against my ass. I guess he's just a man and there's only so much he can control. I feel horny, too, so I unzip my jeans, guide his hand between my legs, and rub his fingers over my clit.

He wakes up and starts to rub me, slowly pushing his fingertips into my pussy. I let my wetness coat his fingers as they slide in and out of me. I roll over and kiss his lips. I never kiss. Just a rule I got about not getting too personal with the tricks. Tommy cups my face and his thick, soft tongue finds mine and intertwines. I pull away from him.

"Why are you treating me like this?" I ask him.

"Because you deserve to be," he says as he stares into my eyes, kissing me again.

Damn, I can't believe how wet that makes me feel, hearing him say that. I pull off my pants and panties and let Tommy make love to me again. Tommy's dick is so big that it makes me exhale when it goes into me. The first time we had sex it was just fucking, albeit very good fucking—the best I've ever had—but this time it's different. This time he makes me feel like I'm the only woman in the world.

Tommy finds my G spot deep inside of me, making me skip every other breath. I move my hips up and down to match his tempo. I swear my clit is on fire it feels so good. I'm not the loud type, but somehow he brings it out of me. I can feel my juices run all over as he works my middle so deeply.

"Oh God . . . Ahhhh . . ." I moan as he makes me climax again, something that no dude has ever taken the time to do. Tears fill my eyes as strange and overwhelming emotions mingle with the sensation of my orgasm. I want it to last forever, but it's too good to be true. Shit like this only happens in the movies. I bet if Nikki could hear me now she'd say I'm talking real soft.

NICOLE "NIKKI" BELL

I can't believe I fucked this nigga all night with no condom. I know he pulled out and busted on me, but that's still playing with fire. I gotta be more careful, but sometimes I'm so caught up that I be wanting to feel that dick raw dog. Besides, Damien be knocked out after fucking this good pussy all night. That makes it easier to take a couple of extra Ben Franklins off his money clip.

Look at this trick. Gave him a little head before he busted that last nut, and I got him sucking his thumb like a baby. This New York nigga ain't had no Southern pussy like this before. Damien might come off like a hardcore thug, but behind closed doors this nigga is a straight trick! I got him eating this good pussy and loving it. Plus, he got paper. The way him and his crew came into town and started flipping weight like pancakes is crazy. These niggas be having that pure shit, not like that shitty stuff Dre's crew be slinging.

I use to fuck with Dre back in the day, back when he was just a corner boy hustling on the block. Back then, he was a minor hustler in Bankhead, and he used to buy shit for me all the time. That nigga was on my clit, trying to get at me, but I didn't pay him any mind. It wasn't until he got the nerve to smoke Manny, the biggest hustler on Southside Atlanta, and took over the trap. Then I started to give him a little dance here and there in the club. Shit, after that, nigga started to hit me off with ice and cash. That's when I gave him some ass. Even then I used to ration it out to him. Had that nigga sprung!

But when Damien came into town he had some real paper. He wasn't just pushin' that nickel-and-dime shit like Dre. He was pushing snow by the kilo. Lucky for me, Damien had a fetish for big-assed, dark-skin girls. Had his tongue all in my ass the first night I fucked him. This nigga breaks me off with rings and shopping sprees. That's why I got my little cousin Mo'Nique down with his boy Tommy. Shit, as fine as she is, she'll have him trickin' all his paper.

As soon as I brought her in the game and had her dancing at The Pink Palace, she was making mad dough! I gotta admit, I'm fine, but Mo be having bitches sweating her ass. Some of them be wanting to get with her and take her home and shit, but she got her silly little strictly dickly rule. Shit, she betta get that paper!

She's a good girl at heart. Sometimes I do feel a little guilty about bringing her into this life, but she's grown now. I ain't keeping her in it. Besides, the money she be making off these tricks be so good. Who's gonna give this up for some bullshit job at Wal-Mart?

With a nigga like Damien breaking me off with two thousand cash every week, this is the best hustle I got. Plus, he got a nice, big dick, even though he only knows how to ram that bitch into me. That's why God gave men tongues. Shit, I be needing my walls licked too! Although he ain't as good at eating pussy as my ex, Andre, he's always good to me. But he's still a trick!

I've heard Dre is getting sick of Damien and his crew locking down College Park and East Point like they is. Plus, the fact I'm fucking Damien now is another reason he don't like him. Dat nigga even said he loved me back in the day when we were fucking. I didn't know if he meant that shit, because most niggas say anything when they about to cum, so I didn't pay any attention to him. Shit, that's his problem if he does.

Same thing goes for Damien's ass too! Shit, the way I hear it, King's the real man behind the Flip Set anyway. He's the real jackpot. I hear Damien talking on the phone with him all the time. He's coming into town next month for some big deal they got going down. If I play my cards right, I'll be sucking his dick and spending his paper soon enough.

Mo'Nique didn't show up at the club tonight. She must be turning Tommy's ass out. Tommy is fine. Too bad he didn't meet me first. Damien's the one calling the shots down here anyway.

The Palace is pretty much an upscale strip club, not like the shithole I use to dance at when I first started. Back in those clubs, anything goes—touching, sucking and fucking—all for the right price. A lot of dudes would pay good money to see or even be a part of some girl-on girl-action. I've had my share, too. In this business you don't have any sexual orientation. Pussy, dick, and ass can all get fucked.

Although they don't get down like that on the main floor, the VIP room is another story.

Mo's lucky she came straight up into The Palace instead of the way I came in the game.

So far tonight, I've already done a few table dances and made about $430. The trick is taking these niggas to the point where they about to bust a nut then leave them wanting more. Now it's time for the big money.

"Hey, Nikki, you ready to go on?" Penny asks me.

"Yeah, all right."

The lights get dim in the Palace and R. Kelly's "Your Body's Callin'" starts to play. I walk out from behind the curtain and command the stage. I roll my waist to the music, and niggas can't stop stuffing bills into my G-string. Niggas just love the way I jiggle my ass.

While I'm dancing, I see Dre watching me from a table. Shit. I'm glad Damien ain't here tonight or there might be some drama.

I continue to dance and finish up my number. I walk over to his table after I'm done.

"What's up, girl?" Dre says in his deep, Southern drawl.

"Same old thing, Dre. What are you doing here?" I ask him.

"I came to see you."

"Well, here I am."

"Yeah, and you still look fine as hell," he says with lust in his voice.

"And you still look good too. So what else is new?"

"Ya know I still got love for you, girl. You still messing with that New York nigga?" he asks.

"Dre, we ain't together anymore. Who I see is my business."

"I know. I just don't know what you see in dat nigga."

"Dre, if you came here to talk about this then I gotta go. I gotta make some money." I start to get up, and he grabs my hand.

"Hold up, Nikki. I'm talking about business too."

I stop and sit back down. "What business you talking about?" I ask him.

"I'm talking about you, me, and this." Dre pulls out a fat roll of hundreds. It's at least a grand. Now, I haven't fucked with Dre in over a year, and now that I'm with Damien, I don't even look in his direction, but a C-note makes me give him a second glance. I pick up the cash and look at him.

"You know I can't leave with you," I tell him.

"Then where?" he asks.

"Follow me."

I take him upstairs and hit the doorman with a hundred to keep him quiet. We go inside a private room. The lights are low, and I lock the door behind us.

Dre unzips his pants and pulls out the big, black dick that I know so well. I sit on the couch as Dre steps in front of me. I take his dick with one hand and slip it in my mouth, sucking him real slow. To be honest, Damien's dick tastes better, but I fake enjoy Dre's anyway.

"Oh, yes, baby. . . . You missed daddy's dick, didn't you?" Dre says to me.

I don't even respond to his corny ad-libs. I speed up my pace trying to get him to the point of cumming. Then I stop.

"Oh, shit, baby!"

I don't want his salty cum in my mouth all night.

"Give me some dick, baby," I say to him.

Dre puts on a rubber from his pocket and I pull off my thong. I lay back and spread my pussy lips with my fingers as Dre pushes his dick inside of me.

"Damn, baby. . . ." Dre loves how tight and warm my pussy is and can't get enough of me. Dre pumps me slow at first, enjoying the feel of my tight walls, then after five minutes, he starts to pump me like a power driver.

"Oh, ssshhhit!" Dre is lost in the sauce like a dope fiend getting a hit after going through withdrawal. Dre busts a nut in the condom and lies on top of me, shaking.

"Damn, I missed your ass, Nikki. You need to stop playing and get back with me."

"We'll see, Dre," I say to make him happy so that he'll get up off me and leave. Dre pulls himself together and gets up, throwing the used condom in the trashcan.

"I'm gonna call you, Nikki."

"All right."

Dre walks out, and I count my money. Dre is such an easy trick. If he thinks I'm leaving Damien, he's more stupid than I thought, but if he keeps hitting me off like this, he can get some ass anytime.

DAMIEN

I ride over to the spot in my Lincoln Navigator with Nikki to check up on Horse. Horse is like an animal let out of his cage. I think he felt more comfortable locked up in Rikers. I guess when ya locked up for 14 years you take that hood mentality with ya. I mean, this nigga got locked up in '91. What was hot back then? Big Daddy Kane, Karl Kani and *New Jack City*? This must be some surreal shit for him. That nigga is hard as hell. This nigga look like a cross between Beanie Sigal and Craig Mack.

I pull up to the corner and roll down the window. Horse walks up.

"What up, son?" Horse says.

"What up, Horse? What's poppin'?"

"The corner's been jumping off something serious."

"You got them young niggas in check?"

"Yeah, son, I got these niggas on the block like clockwork," Horse assures me. He looks over at Nikki sitting next to me. She looks sexy in her shorts and baby doll tee. I don't think this nigga's gotten any pussy since he's been out.

"You got something for me, nigga?" I ask him.

"Yeah, here you go." Horse passes me a brown bag. Enclosed is a rubber-banded stack of money.

"It's about four *G*s," Horse tells me.

"All right."

"Yo, when we heading back up to N.Y., son?" he asks.

"As soon as King says he ready to close the deal with this new, big-time supplier outta L.A. He'll call us," I tell him.

"All right, one."

"Peace."

We pull off. I look over and see Nikki with her face all screwed tight.

"What's wrong, ma?" I ask her.

"I don't like the way that fat nigga be staring at me," Nikki says, disgusted.

"Who, Horse? That nigga all right."

"If you say so. He looks like he ain't never seen no bitch before," Nikki says.

"Come on, ma. He's been locked up for a few joints. Then he sees a woman looking as good as you. . . . How you think he gonna act?"

"I guess, but if he needs some pussy that bad, I'll put him on with some girls at the club. Long as he stop looking at me," Nikki says, revolted.

"Shit, you know some chicks that'll fuck with Horse's big, ugly ass?"

"For the right price, I know some girls that'll fuck him like he's Tyson Beckford!" Nikki says with a laugh.

"Damn, ma, that's cold," I say, laughing.

"So, what's up with ya boy Tommy? What he saying about my cousin Mo?"

"I don't know. I ain't talk to him in a minute now. I think he got ya cousin hemmed up in his bed somewhere getting crazy."

"You might be right. She ain't been at The Palace since the other night. Mo must be putting it on his ass," Nikki says.

"True, but I need some of your fine ass too."

"You know this pussy is all yours, baby. I just need to buy a little something to show it off to you in."

I reach down and peel about seven Ben Franklins off and hand it to her. "Here's a little something for you to go spend."

"Thank you, baby." She reaches over and kisses my cheek.

I take Nikki back to the crib and bust a nut off in her ass. Afterward, I call Tommy to see what's been up with him. He's been spending a lot of time with Mo'Nique the past couple days. Not that I blame him. I'd be up in that ass all the time too.

"What's up, nigga?"

"What's up, Dame?" Tommy says over the phone.

"Damn, nigga, you can't call or something? Mo must be blowing your mind, huh?"

"Yeah, nigga, something like that."

"That young, tight pussy must be like a dream!"

"Nigga, you wildin'. What's going on?" Tommy asks.

"I been talking to King and telling him about how on point you are, and my nigga wants to meet ya."

"Word?"

"Yeah, son, we got big plans going down, man. You ready to make this money?"

"No doubt."

"All right, I'm gonna hit you up later, all right?"

"All right, man." Tommy hangs up.

King's gonna be ready for us soon. Horse can hold things down while Tommy and me head up north next month. That dumbfuck, Corey, is gonna think this is the time for him to shine in front of King while I'm gone. I gotta make sure he don't fuck things up. The only problem we got down here is Dre's bitch ass. We gonna have to shut that nigga down soon.

3

Friend or Foe

MO'NIQUE

For the past four weeks I've been staying off and on at Tommy's place. I haven't been dancing at The Palace, either. I can't believe I'm letting myself fall for him. I try not to show my feelings too much because maybe he does this with all the girls he messes with—treats them good for a month or two, then kicks them to the curb. He gives me money to pay for my T-Mobile bill even though I don't ask him for any. I've been thinking about what we've been discussing, about doing something different with my life. I'm 20 years old. Do I really wanna be stripping when I'm thirty?

I've looked on the Internet at different classes I could take to complete my GED, but I'm kinda scared to do it. What if I fail? What then?

Back to The Palace? I've been saving some of my money in a savings account. I got about eight thousand ready for a rainy day. I've been so caught up in hustling these tricks with Nikki I haven't thought too much about the future. That is, until I met Tommy.

It's like there's a part of him he's keeping from me. Like there's something deeper that he's not letting on to. I don't press him about it, because if he wants to tell me, he will. Besides, I've learned to not get too deep in other people's business, because you might find out some shit that could get you in trouble.

I walk into the living room and see Tommy flipping through channels on the satellite.

"Whatcha watching?" I ask him.

"Nothing really. Hey, come have a seat. I gotta talk to you," he says.

I sit down on the couch next to him.

"Listen, I might be going out of town soon to handle some business in New York," he tells me.

"Oh, okay."

"I know we haven't talked about what's going on between us, and I know you got a night job, so I ain't gonna stop you from doing what you do."

"That's okay. I haven't been exactly doing my job lately."

"Yeah . . . not that I mind," he says, smiling.

"Listen, Tommy, I don't know what's going on between us. I . . . I've been rethinking a lot of things in my life. To be honest with you, I wasn't planning on kickin' it with you like this, but I don't know. Maybe I'm getting ahead of myself."

"Mo'Nique, I wasn't planning on doing this either. Especially with my line of work. It's, um, not a good idea. There are things about me you don't know. Things I can't really talk about with you right now. I want to, I mean, with you here . . ."

"You weren't planning on making a stripper-slash-ho a housewife? I get it." I get up off the couch.

"Mo'Nique." Tommy grabs my hand. "I've never treated you like a ho. I do care about you. I just don't want you to get hurt being with me," he says.

God, I should just walk out now and avoid all this shit. But I can't. Instead I let my guard down.

"I think it would hurt more if I weren't with you."

Tommy pulls me close and kisses my lips, and I get butterflies in my stomach. This is crazy. I ain't supposed to be having feelings like this for no trick. The problem is, I haven't been treating

him like a trick since the night we met. I haven't
had a boyfriend since I was a teenager, since
before James fucked me up. Since that night, I
thought of all men like predators just waiting to
take advantage of me, but Tommy treats me so
good that I can't help but want him.

After I leave Tommy's place, I go home and
see Nikki and Penny sitting on the couch.

"Well, well, well, look who decided to come
back home," Nikki remarks.

"Hey, what's up, y'all?" I say to them as I walk
by.

"Damn, girl, is the dick that good? You hav-
en't been at The Palace in weeks. I hope you got
Tommy's wallet open."

"Nikki, don't worry about it. I know what I'm
doing."

Nikki gets a strange look on her face, and I
walk to my room. She gets up and follows me.

"Oh, no, girl, you startin' to really feel this
nigga, ain't ya?"

"Nikki, please," I say, irritated.

"You are!" Nikki says with shock as she comes
and sits on my bed. "What did I tell you about
catching feelings for these niggas? Don't put
yourself through it, Mo," she tells me.

"Tommy's different. He's not like the other
guys I used to mess with."

"Mo, Tommy is a hustler just like Damien. He's probably got another bitch he's sleeping with. Just get the money and move on, girl."

"Nikki, it's not like that. Trust me."

"Oh God, I thought I taught you better than to go catching feelings for a trick. I guess you just gotta find out the hard way. Anyways, I got us a party next month up in Bankhead that Trey-D is throwing. Says there's gonna be a lot of money there for us to make. You, me, and Penny can clean up."

"I don't know," I tell her.

"You don't know? Shit, girl, you better wake up and face reality. This ain't *Pretty Woman*! Tommy don't give a fuck about you, and he ain't paying your bills either."

"All right, Nikki! Shit! I'll think about it, okay?"

"Whatever. Don't do me any favors. Just more money for me and Penny." Nikki gets up and walks out.

"Girl thinking a nigga gonna take care of her! She need to get her mind right!" Nikki says to Penny. Maybe she's right. I can't be that lucky.

JAYSON

I drive to the spot out in Decatur to meet with Lt. McNiven. It's been three weeks since I last checked in, and I can tell he feels uncomfortable with me being undercover for this long. When most undercover cops are in this long, they start to take on the traits of the character they're playing. I can't say that I haven't gotten used to this life. The sad thing is, it's actually better in some ways than my real life. I haven't been called Jayson Harper in so long that I've almost forgotten the name, but as far as losing myself to Tommy Holloway, it's not gonna happen.

"Harper, how you doing?" McNiven asks me.

"I'm good."

"What's going on with Damien?" he asks.

"I'm gonna meet the King," I say.

"When?"

"Sometime next month. We're supposed to be flying up north so Damien can introduce me."

"Okay, I'm gonna make sure to have a contact already in place for you. How much does Damien trust you?" he asks.

"He trusts me. If he didn't, I wouldn't get anywhere near King. No one has ever been this deep. I can get him."

"How come you're so sure?"

"I don't know the details yet, but King is working on some big deal. His operations are gonna go beyond New York and Atlanta. He's already making moves in Virginia and North Carolina.

If we wanna arrest him for more than tax evasion, now is the time."

"Okay, you know these people. I trust your judgment. How are you feeling other than this?" McNiven asks.

"I'm fine, Lieutenant."

"So I hear. Who's the girl?" he asks with concern.

"You know about her?" I say, surprised.

"She's been practically living in your place for three weeks now. What do you think?"

"Mo'Nique's a good girl."

"That you met through Damien. She could be there to watch you."

"I haven't blown my cover. She's not an issue."

"Jayson, listen. I know you're going through a rough divorce, but don't get caught up with this girl. You don't know anything about her. Don't let her get in your head."

"She's not," I lie.

"Good, because I will pull you out if I see any signs that you're not focused," he warns me.

"You don't have to worry about that." I turn, walk back to my car, and get in. As I pull out, I can't help but think that maybe he's right. Maybe she's better than I thought. Maybe I'm being worked over by a smarter hustler.

*****

That night, I go with Mo'Nique, Quan, Horse, Corey, Nikki, and Damien to see a concert at the Georgia Dome. The show features T.I., Ludacris, Keyshia Cole, and Young Jeezy. It's a hood fest. Every wannabe hustler, thug, baller, pimp, ho, groupie, and rapper is in the house.

"That's my nigga, T.I.," Damien says.

"Thought you didn't like these down south niggas?" I say to him.

"Naw, I don't like these down south niggas that are hustling on my corners. T.I. and Jeezy be spitting that hustling shit," he explains.

"Well, Luda is nicer than people give him credit for," Quan says.

"That crazy shit he be saying? Man, I wanna hear that Dipset shit!" Corey yells.

"There's more to hip-hop than hustlin' and thuggin'," Quan argues.

"Nigga, go 'head wit' that backpack shit. Ain't nobody listening to that bullshit!" Corey barks back.

"Shut the fuck up and stop yelling in my ear! I can't hear the damn music!" Damien yells at him.

Mo'Nique and Nikki are standing near the stage. I can't help but think that she's playing me. Can I really trust her?

***

NIKKI

This show is the shit and so is T.I.! I gave him a lap dance once at Magic City and was this close to getting him when they had to bounce. Damn shame. I could've made a lot of cash and fucked his fine ass.

I look behind me and see Horse's ugly ass staring at my shit like a cheeseburger or something. I wish this nigga would go beat his dick somewhere and leave me alone!

I was a little rough on Mo the other day. I just didn't expect her to fall for Tommy like that. When I was younger, I fell for a trick too. This nigga promised me all kinds of shit—he'd take care of me, he'd buy me this or do that. The nigga played me. Never again will I let myself get played out like that. I don't want Mo to go through the same thing I went through, especially after what that bitch-ass stepfather did to her, but I gotta make it up to her.

"Mo, I'm sorry about the other night, girl. You know I was just trippin', right?"

"Yeah, I know," she says.

"Listen, Mo, if you really feeling Tommy like that, I ain't gonna throw salt in your game."

"Thank you, Nikki. I do know what I'm doing."

"I know, girl. I taught you well." She smiles and we continue to dance to T.I.

Between me and Mo'Nique, ain't no other bitches in here that can fuck with us. I'm wearing my white, skintight Prada dress and matching Gucci pumps. Mo has on a black Prada dress and some Dolce & Gabbana stilettos. We're both breaking it down while Damien and Tommy stand behind us. There are plenty of men watching us, but nobody dares to step. Damien is known and respected by niggas. The only nigga that don't give a fuck about Damien is Dre, who happens to be standing to the right of us about eight rows up. Quan sees Dre watching me dance and lets Damien know.

"Yo, Dame. To your right, dog," Quan tells Damien.

"Tommy, Horse, look at that fucking nigga over there," Damien says, pissed. I don't want shit to get ugly here. I know both Damien and Dre are strapped and that both of them won't hesitate to blast the other here.

"Damien, don't do nothing to him, not here," I plead.

"Nikki, stay over here." Damien ignores me.

Thankfully, Tommy chimes in as the voice of reason.

"Dame, we pull out on them niggas here we gonna cause a riot and five-o is gonna lock us up. You see the security in here?" Tommy says.

"I don't give a fuck about no five-o! This nigga gotta get snuffed!" Damien yells.

"Nikki, come on, let's go," Mo'Nique says to me as she pulls my arm.

"I know you don't, but King needs us here, not locked up," Tommy reminds him.

Damien looks at Tommy, nods his head, and falls back. I breathe a sigh of relief. We go back to enjoying the concert. Damien whispers something in Horse's ear and he nods. I got a feeling Damien isn't going to let it go so easily.

After the show, we walk out to the parking garage, but Horse isn't with us. I have a really bad feeling in my gut that something is gonna go down. Damien's walking quickly to the truck, and I'm right behind him. Tommy and Mo'Nique get in his car, while Quan and Corey get into their car. As we pull out of the garage, we hear six shots bang out. Damien pulls up to the corner quick, and Horse runs to the truck.

"Hurry the fuck up and get in!" Damien yells at Horse.

"What the fuck did you do?" I shout at Damien, but he doesn't answer me.

"Did you blast that nigga?" Damien barks at Horse as he peels off.

"Naw, this other little ma'fucker got in the way and caught it!"

"Fuck! You can't shoot worth shit, nigga!"

"You fuckin' shoot him then!" Horse yells back.

"Oh my God," I say in shock.

Tommy and Quan follow us onto I-75 South as we speed down the highway.

It turns out Horse shot and killed Dre's cousin, Rodney. Shit was already bad between them, but now I know shit is gonna be fucked up. Dre is gonna go to war with Damien, fo'sho! Damn, these dumb tricks are messing up my hustle with this bullshit!

DAMIEN

Damn! This nigga Horse can't shoot straight to save his life! Dre is gonna try and get back at me. I can't believe this shit. I give that big, ugly, Oreo cookie-eating muthafucka one mutha-fuckin' job to do and he fucks it up. How hard is it to murder a nigga? I shoulda handled that shit myself.

We all get back to my spot in College Park.

"What the fuck happened back there, man?" Tommy yells at me.

"Horse can't fucking aim," I say.

"I told you it was crowded!" Horse barks.

"I thought I told you to wait! Shit!" Tommy yells.

"I run this shit, Tommy. I don't need your permission to do shit!" I remind him.

"You shoulda let me do it. I woulda split that nigga's wig with one shot!" Corey boasts.

"Shut the fuck up!" Horse yells.

"Don't be mad, nigga, 'cause you can't shoot," Corey says to Horse.

Horse pulls out his nine. "I'll show you how good I can aim, nigga," Horse says.

Corey pulls out his .45. "Come on, nigga! Do something!" Corey shouts back.

"Both of y'all bitches shut up," I yell at them. "Now just calm down. Y'all head out to the spot and make sure them bitches don't try something out there," I tell them. They all just stand there looking at each other. "Now!" I yell.

They walk to the car and get in. Tommy stands there and looks at me.

"What, nigga?"

"Dame, this didn't have to go down like this," Tommy says.

"But it did, all right? Sometimes you can't play it safe, Tommy. You gotta show these niggas it ain't no game."

"All right, man."

"Tommy, listen, these niggas ain't shit. Besides, we got more important things to attend to. King called me and said for us to fly up tomorrow, so go home, pack ya shit, tap Mo'Nique's pretty ass, and meet me here tomorrow at eleven, all right?" I reassure him.

"All right," Tommy says, still unconvinced.

"Trust me, Tommy, this ain't nothing."

Tommy nods his head and walks over to Mo'Nique in the car and they drive off. Tommy is a smart nigga. We need niggas like him down with us.

I walk inside and see Nikki calming her nerves with some Armadale Vodka.

"You all right, ma?"

"Yeah, I just needed to drink a little something," Nikki says then takes a swig.

"Cool. Why don't you pour me one too."

Nikki pours out a drink for me. I knock it back in two shots.

"I'm gonna miss ya, ma, while I'm gone."

"Me too, baby," Nikki says.

"Why don't you give me a little something to remember ya by?"

Nikki smiles, turns around, faces the bar, and pulls her thong down. I pull her dress up around her waist. I love that fat ass of hers. I slide my two fingers between her legs and rub her twat.

"That feels good, daddy," Nikki says.

"You been keeping your pussy tight for me?"

"Only you, daddy. Ahhh . . ."

I push my fingers inside and finger fuck her. For a girl that pops her pussy all night, she sure keeps it tight. Reminds me of my baby mama up north, although she don't got an ass this fat.

"You want some dick, baby?"

"Yeah, daddy, give me that good dick," Nikki begs.

I unzip my pants, pull my dick out, and push it in from behind. Nikki bends over farther and gives me that ass. I love the way her brown ass looks when I'm pumping that pussy daddy-long-dick style.

Nikki's ass is so soft and round that it jiggles like jelly when I hit it from the back. I know a lot of other niggas done already ran up in this ass, but I bet they ain't never fuck her as good as this. Besides, I've been the only nigga fucking this pussy for the past five months, so I know it's good and tight.

After about fifteen minutes, I pull up out of her and skeet on her ass. Damn . . . I love watching that shit run down the crack of her ass.

"Go clean up, baby."

"You gonna give me some more of that dick later, daddy?"

"Damn right. I just wanted to get that first nut outta the way. I'm gonna blow ya back out, ma."

"Ooohh, I'll be waiting for you," Nikki says as she walks into the bathroom. I love these Atlanta freaks.

MO'NIQUE

As we drive back to Tommy's house, I can tell he's upset. When we get in the house, he goes in his room and starts to pack his suitcase.

"You're leaving tomorrow," I say to him.

"Yeah, I should be back in a week or so."

"Are you all right?"

"That was just some dumb, unnecessary shit tonight," Tommy says, pissed.

I don't know what to say to him. He turns and looks at me. "Listen, you can stay here while I'm gone and drive the car."

"You don't have to do that, Tommy." I can't believe I just said that.

"It's okay. I trust you."

"Okay, just promise me you're gonna be careful."

"I will, baby."

I don't want him to go, but I know he's got no choice. I just have a feeling that he's gonna be in danger up there. I've never worried so much for a man like I do for Tommy.

We make love that night. The whole time, I cling on to him as if it's the last time I'll feel his body against mine. In the morning, I drop him off at Damien's and go back to his place. I can't help but feel depressed. I think to myself that I want to do something different with my life. Dancing at The Pink Palace isn't a future. It's time for a new hustle.

I guess some things are easier said than done. The next night, I'm back at The Pink Palace. It's business as usual. The only thing different is me. For some reason I can't figure out, I'm just not feeling it. Spending the past couple of weeks with Tommy has made me feel as if I could do anything with my life, but I have to face reality. I have bills to pay.

I see Nikki back in the dressing room putting on her makeup. "What's up, Nikki?"

"Hey, Mo," she says as she looks at me in the mirror. "So how you been since Tommy left?"

"All right, I guess," I say sadly.

"That's how it is when you open yourself to a man. They always leave. Especially men like Tommy. Messing with hustlers ain't always the fairy-tale we want it to be."

"So, is that the reason you don't open yourself up to Dre?" I ask her. Nikki stops and looks at me, and I know I hit a nerve.

"Dre is a trick and that's all he'll ever be to me," she says seriously.

"Okay, if you say so. Have you heard from him since his cousin Rodney got killed?"

"No. I knew Damien was gonna do something stupid. These dumb niggas don't know how to act," Nikki says as she gets up from her chair.

"Nikki, Damien is crazy. Maybe you should cut that nigga loose. You know as soon as he comes back, Dre is gonna come after him," I say.

"Mo, I got Damien under control. And Dre knows if he comes after Damien he'll kill him. He ain't stupid."

"Come on, Nikki, you know how Dre is. I just don't wanna see you get caught in the crossfire like Rodney did."

"You worry too much, Mo. Besides, Dre wouldn't let anything happen to me. Look, Damien might not even come back. Tommy might not either. That's why I don't let my feelings get involved with these tricks. Listen, I gotta get out there and make these tricks pay up. I'll talk to you later, all right?" Nikki says as she walks to the stage entrance.

"Yeah, okay."

Oh my God, what if she's right? What if Tommy doesn't come back? All this time I've been worried about him getting killed, I never thought about what I'd do if he just decided to stay up there. Who am I kidding? I'm not that important to him. I'm just some ho working at a strip club. Welcome back to reality, Mo'Nique.

After Nikki goes on stage, I decide to do a couple of table dances. There are a few regulars in the club tonight. My main inhouse trick, Mike, a.k.a. Snaggle Puss, is on the couch with his boys, Lew and Pat. They call themselves the Royal Blue Crew for some reason. I really don't care why they call themselves that. All I know is that they are some big ballers that tip well.

"What's up, Snaggle? What you in the mood for tonight?" I teasingly ask him.

"Oh, you know what I want, shorty. I been dying to see you again," Mike says as he pulls out a fifty.

"I know. You gonna tell me why they call you Snaggle Puss tonight?"

"I can show you better than I can tell you. . . . oh, shit," Mike says as I turn around and show him my fat ass in my red thong.

"I bet you can."

"You see, that's why I can't get enough of you, Mo'Nique. Damn." Mike and his crew are awestruck by the way I roll my ass and grind my waist to the beat.

T-Pain's "I'm N Love Wit A Stripper" bumps over the loudspeakers. I arch my back and pop my ass like a freak in heat until I have them all coming out the nose with money. I undo the straps of my bikini and let my top fall slowly. First my right nipple says peek-a-boo, and then my left does the same, as Mike's tongue hangs out of his face like a dog's. Pretty soon, I see a hundred dollar bill being stuffed in my thong as Mike's fingers try to get a free sample of my goodies. I turn around just in time, pulling his finger out and leaving the money in. Now I see why they call him Snaggle Puss, sneaky mutherfucka!

By the time the song ends, I get at least $1,100 out of the Royal Blue Crew. "Thank you, boys," I say as I walk away.

"Damn, she the finest girl up in here," I hear Mike tell his boys. Maybe I should just forget about Tommy and go back to hustling these tricks like Nikki said I should do. It's pretty obvious Tommy's forgotten about me. I go back to the dressing room and open my locker. My Helio buzzes with a new text message:

Hey, just wanted you 2 know that I miss U and I'm gonna be back soon. I can't stop thinking about you.

Luv U.

-Tommy

Damn, just when I thought it was all a fluke, he goes and does this. I can't stop smiling. After I get his message, I leave the club and go home. Besides, I already made enough for the night. I'm gonna send Tommy some naked pictures of me. I'm gonna remind him of what he's missing down here so that he'll hurry back.

4

Deep cover

Jamaica, Queens, New York

JAYSON

This is my first time in New York. Damien and I arrive at five p.m. and take a taxi to King's home in Jamaica, Queens. His place is more like a mansion than a house. Damien tells me that he paid seven million for the estate.

King's rise to the top of New York's drug dealer food chain is nothing short of remarkable. He gave "hostile takeover" a new meaning by the way he locked things down when he got out of prison in '97.

As we pull into the white mansion's circular driveway, all I can think about is how nobody's ever been this deep before. Damien and I knock on the door, and a maid comes to show us in. This cat has money for real.

"Hey, Dame, so how much is it all worth?"

"What do you mean?" he looks at me and asks.

"The empire," I clarify.

"Hmmm, roughly about seventy mil," he says.

"Damn, I can dig that," I say as we walk through the marble foyer.

We enter into King's huge living room. It's decorated in hardwood with handmade tables and chairs that look too expensive to sit in. We walk through two double doors and into another big room, where we see Dwayne "King" Smith sitting on a huge black leather sofa. He's watching the Knicks play the Spurs on a Samsung fifty-inch widescreen plasma TV. King is a light-skinned nigga with a freshly shaven fade. He holds a blunt in his hands.

"What's up, my nigga?" King says to Damien as he gets up off the sofa and gives him a man-hug.

"What's up, King?" Damien says.

"You looking sharp, nigga," King remarks.

"You know how I do. Yo, this is my man, Tommy Holloway," Damien says.

"So, you're Tommy? I heard good things about ya, man," King says.

"I heard the same about you," I reply.

"Damien says you a real thoroughbred nigga. You saved Dame's life."

"I just did what I had to do."

"You know, we don't really fuck with niggas we don't know, but if Dame says you down, that carries weight," King says.

"Damien says that you're the one to be down with to make this money," I say.

"Well, look around. What do you think?" King asks me.

"I think you doing major things," I tell him.

"So how's the spot down there?" King asks Dame.

"Yo, it's nonstop, my nigga," Damien reveals.

King walks back to the sofa and sits down. "Sit down," King tells us. We sit on the sofa. King takes a puff off his blunt and then passes it to Damien.

"So, you know this deal I got working on with these cats out in L.A. is gonna make us a huge amount of money," King tells us.

Damien passes the blunt to me. "That sounds good, nigga," Damien says.

"What about the police and the ATF?" I ask him.

King chuckles and looks at me. "Damien was right; you do think ahead. We got the police in our back pocket. Let's just say that there are certain high-ranking officers and prosecutors who'll be getting a large check as soon as the deal is complete," King says.

This guy is no small-time thug. If what he's saying is true, he's better connected than we thought.

As King begins to reveal his plans to us, the double doors open, and standing there is a beautiful woman dressed in a blue striped silk dress with matching open-toed shoes. Her skin is a smooth, honey brown hue, and her dress hugs her curvy and well-toned body. She wears a simple silver necklace with a diamond charm hanging from it.

My heart feels like it's dancing on my tongue. My pulse jumps. It isn't because of her obvious beauty that I'm bugging out. It's because I know this woman, and more importantly, she knows me. Her name is Vanessa Wells, and she was my girlfriend from high school twelve years ago.

"Yo, this is my better half, Vanessa, Tommy," King says. I look in her eyes and she looks into mine. I'm a dead man. No ifs, ands, or buts about it. She knows me as Jayson Harper. My only other option now is to pull out my piece and maybe shoot my way out of here.

To my surprise, Vanessa plays a different hand. "Nice to meet you, Tommy," she says.

"You too," I nervously reply.

"What's up, Dame?" Vanessa says.

"Hey, Vanessa," Damien shoots back.

This is unreal. Why does she, of all people, have to be here with him? The woman I was so in love with back in the day is here now. I know she recognizes me.

"Baby, I didn't mean to interrupt you, but I wanted to know if we were still going to your mother's tonight," Vanessa says.

King gets an uneasy look on his face. "Uh, listen, we got some things we need to discuss. We can reschedule for another night," King says.

"Okay, but you know how your mother is."

"I'll call her, all right?"

"Whatever. It's your mother," Vanessa says as she walks out. "Tommy, it's nice to have met you." She closes the door and King laughs.

"Women. Don't ever settle down, niggas. They can be so demanding. It takes a real man to handle them," King says.

"You don't even gotta worry about that, nigga," Damien says and puffs the blunt.

We drink and smoke for the rest of night until about eleven o'clock. Damien decides to go check on his son up in Harlem, and King stays up to watch The Wire on HBO. He says that he's addicted to the show.

I go upstairs and settle into a room on the west side of the building. I lie on the bed with my gun under my pillow, in case things get ugly.

I can't sleep. How can Vanessa be here? We were together our whole senior year. We were in love with each other. The last time I saw her was before she left to go to NYU after high school. We tried the whole long-distance thing, but it never worked out. I married Lauren two years after we broke up, but I always wondered how Vanessa was doing. I never thought she would end up here.

Will she blow my cover to King? Does she know I'm a cop? As I'm thinking of different scenarios on how to get out of this alive, I hear a knock on the door. I grab my gun and take the safety off.

"Who is it?"

"It's me," Vanessa says.

I rest my hand under my pillow, still holding on to my gun. "Come in," I say, uneasy about what's about to happen.

Vanessa walks in and closes the door behind her. We stare at each other in an uncomfortable silence.

"What are you doing here, Jayson?"

"I could ask you the same question," I reply.

"I think you're in more of an awkward position than me. Why are you calling yourself Tommy?" she asks.

"Vanessa, you know why. And you know why I'm here, too," I say. I stare into her eyes and she immediately knows what I mean.

"Oh my God, do you have any idea what he'll do to you if he finds out?"

"Yeah, I got a good idea. The more important question, however, is are you gonna tell him?"

"Jayson, this is me you're talking to. You know me. I wouldn't do that to you."

"The Vanessa I knew wouldn't be sleeping with Scarface downstairs either. What are you doing with him, Vanessa?"

Vanessa looks away then gathers her thoughts. "A lot has changed since high school, Jayson. It's not as black and white as you think," she says.

"Explain it to me then."

"Things happened in my life I couldn't control. I . . . got caught up in some things and Dwayne helped me out," Vanessa says to me regretfully.

"So what, now you're paying him back?"

"When you get involved with a man like Dwayne, you can't walk away so easily. How long does he have?" she asks.

"As soon as this deal he's planning is completed."

"And what happens to me?" she asks as she stares in my eyes.

"If you're not involved, nothing."

Vanessa breathes in relief. "It's good to see you again, Jayson." She turns and leaves the room. Damn, this shit has just gotten even more complicated.

DAMIEN

I'm driving to my BM's house out in Harlem at about midnight. I love being back up here. This is my town. Back when I was a kid running these streets, I used to look up to the major hustlers. I was dying to be just like them. I used to be a corner boy, hustling all night long. King put me on and brought me into Da Untouchables with Bishop and got me hustling for real, making money. Now look at us. We run this city. We got most of New York on lock.

Those were the days. The '90s were off the chain. That's when things were hot, for real. Can't help but think of my girl, Stacy, back then. She was the only girl that ever really got to me, until her trifling ass started messing with that nigga, Remo, in Brooklyn. That's when I realized you couldn't trust any of these hoes. The only bitch I got any real love for is my baby momma, Trina. She's a real downass chick, not just because she had my baby, but because she always had my back.

I pull up to my Trina's brownstone and park, then walk to the front and knock on the door.

"Who is it?" Trina says. I know she sees me through the peephole.

"It's me. Open up."

Trina opens the door dressed in a long T-shirt and head wrap. She looks me up and down.

"You gonna let me in?"

"It's after twelve. What if I had company?"

"You better not have any nigga up in here with my son." I walk by her.

"He's sleeping, Damien."

"I ain't gonna wake him up." I walk to his room and look at my seed sleeping in his tiny racecar bed. Damn, he's gonna grow up and be just like me, only he won't have to run the streets like me. I'm gonna take care of my boy.

I kiss his head, close the door behind me, and walk to Trina's bedroom. She's sitting on her bed watching TV.

"So, who you been fuckin' with up here?"

"Nigga, please. I know you down in Atlanta fucking some freak, so don't be accusing me of shit," she snaps. She's right, but that's not the point.

"Don't worry about what I'm doing. Answer the question," I say to her.

"I ain't messing with nobody here, Damien. If I were, you would already know that."

"Damn right I would. I don't want my seed calling no other nigga Daddy," I tell her.

"Whatever, Damien. What you doing up here?"

"Just handling some business."

"Well, you can handle some business here too. Taye need some new clothes. He's outgrowing everything," Trina says.

"You know I'm gonna take care of my seed, ma."

"Okay, whatever." She rolls her eyes.

"Why you acting like that?" I ask her.

"Like what?" she sarcastically retorts.

"Like you ain't happy to see me."

"Should I be?"

"Don't front. You know you want me, ma."

Trina smiles as I caress her right titty through her shirt. That's what I love about Trina—she's a straight project chick, a whole lot of attitude and shit, but she's fine as hell too. She ain't as thick as Nikki, but she's thick in all the right places.

I sit next to her on the bed and kiss her neck. Trina might give me a lot of attitude, but she knows what time it is when I come through.

I slide my hand up her thick brown thighs and play with her pussy under her panties. "Why you always gotta give me a hard time, girl?"

"'Cause you give me one," she says back.

Damn, she gets wet so fast I can feel it through her panties. She raises her hips and I pull her underwear off as she lies back on the bed. I take my pants and boxers off and get on top of her.

"I know you fucking some other bitch down in Atlanta, Damien," Trina says to me unhappily, but still allowing me to rub her wet pussy with my dick.

"You know you're my heart, girl," I say to her as I slide my dick up and down her moist slit. Then I push up in her and tear that ass up.

"Oh . . . give me that dick, Dame," Trina moans out in a Trinidadian accent.

The sex is always live with Trina. She always be on some porno shit when we fuck. It must be that Trinidadian blood running in her veins. Her accent always comes out when we fight or have sex. I think that's what turns me on about her. Plus, that little fat ass of hers makes me wanna bang all night long. Maybe I shouldn't be hitting her ass raw dog, but her shit be so good a nigga can't help but nut up in it. Oh, well. I might as well give, Taye, a little sister or something. I love homecomings.

5

The Last Dance

MO'NIQUE

Tommy's been gone to New York for two weeks now. He called me a day ago and said he didn't know when he would be back; he would call me when he knew. He says he's fine, but I still can't help but worry about him. Nikki calls me every other day, asking when I'm going to come back and dance at The Pink Palace. I keep on telling her not yet, even though I could use the money. Tommy left two grand for me to spend, but I haven't touched it. I don't want him to think I'm using him. I've actually signed up for a course so I can complete my GED. It turns out I only have to pass four tests with a C average or higher.

I've been thinking about my life and what I wanna do with it. I used to love dancing before

I started at The Palace, but now I can't stand it. I like decorating. Maybe I could be an interior designer. I do like to sketch dress designs out on paper, too, but I won't be designing shit if I don't pass this course.

I hear a knock on the door. I get up and answer it. It's Nikki.

"What's up, Nikki?"

"What's up, girl? I see why you've been staying here. This shit is nice," she says as she walks in and f lops down on the couch.

"What's going on, Nikki?"

"Well, I know you're on this new shit with Tommy, but I need your help."

"What is it?"

"Well, you know that party I told you about last month? The one that Trey-D is throwing tomorrow night? Well, I promised him there would be three of us, and when I told him only two of us could make it, he said he'd find some other dancers to take our place."

"So you want me to come with y'all? Nikki, I know how Trey-D's parties get down. I ain't feeling that."

"Girl, please. I wouldn't ask you if it wasn't an emergency," Nikki pleads.

"Why don't you get some other girl from the club?"

"Them bitches? I ain't trying to give them greedy hoes any of my money. Mo, if I show up with you, them niggas are gonna empty out their pockets! Ballers, Mo! You don't have to do anything with them. Just shake a little something then bounce. Please, I need you," Nikki says.

I should say no, but Nikki has always looked out for me, and I do need some money. "All right, just this once," I reluctantly say.

"Thank you, girl! Hey, have you heard from Tommy?" she asks.

"Yeah, just yesterday. Haven't you been talking to Damien?"

"Yeah, girl, you know he be blowing me up all day," Nikki says quickly.

"Anyway, I call you tomorrow and we'll meet up, okay?"

"All right."

I could tell Nikki was lying about the Damien part. He's probably hoeing around up there on her. It's not like Nikki don't do the same behind his back anyway. I don't know what she's gonna to do with her life. She's already twenty-five and she ain't gonna be young forever.

The next night I meet up with Nikki in a nice, closed-gate community in Buckhead. I drive up to a big house in the cut and I see a few Benzes and Escalades parked out front. There must be some rich niggas up in here. I see Nikki and Penny standing out front waiting for me, and I pull up next to them.

"I thought you wasn't gonna show up for a second," Nikki says.

"Just got caught in traffic. We gonna get changed inside?"

"Yeah, girl, we gonna blow these tricks' minds," Nikki says.

For some reason, I can't help but feel degraded by that comment. Are they tricks for giving us money, or are we the ones selling ourselves short? Anyway, we go in the back door and Trey-D shows us to our changing room. I put on my old, plunge halter baby doll teddy with black silk panties. Nikki dresses in a pink two-piece bikini with matching high heel shoes. Penny, who measures at 34-28-42, has on a tan bikini that ties in the back. Penny is a very voluptuous and curvy girl with big titties, thick thighs, and a small enough waist to make it look sexy.

We all put on trench coats and walk out to the living room where there are about twenty corporate-looking types—the kind of guys who work downtown. There are a few niggas dressed in Sean John and Rocawear, but they look like they have money.

The music cuts off, and all three of us stand in the center of the room. Then Shawnna and Ludacris' "Gettin' Some" starts to bump from the stereo. We drop our coats to the floor, making every man groan and gawk at us. We start to break it down to the music.

We all do the standard rump-shaker moves that make our asses bounce. Penny has a talent, if you can call it that, for making one ass cheek shake, then the other, and then both together. The men love it. Nikki is a gyrator, and she pushes her rump up against a man's dick and practically jacks him off with her ass cheeks. Me, I'm a dancer at heart. Nikki tells me that that's a talent most women don't have, and that's what gives me an edge. I grind my hips like a snake and belly dance, then I dip it down low and pop my pussy to the floor. I'm so used to doing it that I don't have to think about it.

The funny thing is, I'm thinking about how much I don't wanna be here. Pretty soon, we all get separated and start to give private dances. The men, for the most part, are respectful and don't try to stick their fingers up in me and shit. They just take tens and twenties and hold them out. I get closer and they push the bills between my panty lining.

I look around. Penny has already taken off her top.She's rubbing her titties in some guy's face while Nikki rides some nigga.

I seem to be getting most of the attention as a small group has formed around me. You can clearly see my round, soft titties through my sheer black teddy. Some men rub their fingers over my firm nipples. One guy is sweating me serious. The music switches to Nelly's "Tip Drill."

The one guy that's sweating me whispers in my ear. "I would love to go somewhere private with you."

I don't reply to him and keep on dancing. Trey-D has four more girls come over, and they start to freak.

The guy who's trying to holla whispers in my ear again. "I got two thousand I can give you if we can go somewhere."

Once again, I ignore him and dance over to another guy standing by the wall. I start to grind my ass on him as he reaches around and stuffs a twenty down the front of my panties. The other dude walks up to me again. Damn, he's persistent.

"What's it gonna take for you to come play with me, baby?" he asks.

"You don't have enough," I tell him and walk away, looking around the room for Nikki. I don't see her. I don't see Penny, either. Great, where are they? I walk to the back room and still don't see them. I head upstairs and look in the bathroom and see nothing. Where the hell are they? I know they didn't just leave my ass here.

As I'm walking down the hallway, I hear a man moan in a nearby room. I push the half-open door and see Nikki and Penny doing some *ménage à trois* shit. Penny's riding some guy's dick reverse cowgirl style, while Nikki's sitting on his face, drowning him with her pussy.

I close the door and walk to the back room. I get my stuff and change back to my street clothes. Nikki and Penny can have this shit. I'm done.

As I walk to my car, the asshole that was trying to holla at me inside runs up.

"Hey, hey, wait up."

"What?" I say, pissed off.

"Listen, I'm willing to make it worth your while. A girl as beautiful as you shouldn't be dancing. I can take care of you, girl. I just wanna be with you," he says with a stupid-ass grin on his face. This dude looks like an uglier version of that pimp that be with Snoop Dogg all the time. I stare at him then start to laugh.

"Listen, I know you think you can flash some money and I'll go with you, and I don't blame you for thinking that. A month ago, I probably would've. But I can't do this shit no more. Besides, I got a man in my life." I turn and walk away. He cusses me out as I drive away, but I don't care.

This is officially the nail in the coffin for me. Tommy's right; I can do a whole lot better than this. I just wish he would come back soon so I could tell him that.

6

Pussy Kills

JAYSON

For the past three weeks, I've been in New York with Damien, getting close to King and gaining his trust. It hasn't been easy seeing Vanessa and King together. What trouble could she have been in to make her turn to him? It's pure torture watching a woman I once loved give herself to a man as foul as this nigga. We haven't talked to each other since that first night, but there are times when she looks at me and her eyes seem to be yelling for help.

At the same time, I've been missing Mo'Nique back in Atlanta. I know I shouldn't be feeling this way for her, but I can't help it. Since I've been with her, I've felt brand new and happy. But she knows Tommy the hustler, not Jayson the cop. As soon as this assignment is over, that whole relationship will end. I don't wanna let her go. She's young and has her whole life ahead of her. Why would she want to be with a cop?

King is a slick nigga. He's got these different girls' apartments throughout Harlem that he pays the rent for and sets up shop in. They cook up the product and sell it out of these places. He's even got office buildings in Manhattan that he rents out through different spas and hair salons. They supply the corporate types with nose candy. He also gets a cut out of the "private massages" that the women in the spas offer for the right price. King has evolved beyond a common street thug and doesn't get his hands dirty anymore. Back in the day, King was a ruthless killer that was known for slitting niggas from ear to ear. Nowadays, Damien is his triggerman. King points to a corner, and three niggas die by sunset.

This whole time, King has been watching me, checking me out and making sure I'm as down as Damien says I am. This nigga ain't stupid; but neither am I. This supplier out in L.A. is going to be trafficking their product to him in Atlanta. That's why Damien and the Flip Set have been locking down College Park and East Point for the past six months.

The three of us are kicking it at a nightclub in Harlem called The Blue Angel. Women are all around us, throwing their panties at King. Word is, a big-time hustler called Bishop owned this spot in the '90s. King "inherited" the club after Bishop's untimely death and took over the business.

At the table we have two bottles of Moët and three gold bottles of Cristal. We're getting fucked up. King has this fine-ass chick called Charlene, a bronze-skinned girl with Asian facial features, sitting in his lap. She has on a low-cut dress that goes down to her belly button, showing off the cleavage of her C-cup titties. Her long, silky black hair is pulled to the side and King strokes it with one hand. His other hand is on her inner thigh.

"So you a model, ma?" King asks her.

"Yeah, I do a little," Charlene says.

"Yo, Tommy, this is the life you gonna be enjoying pretty soon," King says to me.

"That's what I'm here for," I tell him.

"Damien tells me you got a bad-ass little red thing down in ATL."

"Yeah, she's straight."

"Good. Just remember you can never have enough pussy, nigga," King says as he palms Charlene's ass.

"No doubt," Damien chimes in.

"Yo, Dame, you still fucking Trina ass raw?" King asks.

"You know that's my boo. That pussy be like crack. You know how that is," Damien says.

I take another drink of Cristal, and lean back and close my eyes.

"Whoa, cowboy, take it easy. Don't pop, nigga," King says when he sees my closed eyes.

"I'm . . . fine, man," I say with a little slur.

"Yo, Dame, get the car and get your man back to the house," King instructs.

"A'ight," Damien says. Damien helps me up, walks me out to the car, and tells the driver to take me back to the mansion.

I wasn't really that drunk. I just wanted to get out of there and clear my head. The house is quiet at three o'clock in the morning. I go to my room and lie on the bed. I'm lost in thought about what I'm going to do. My door opens and Vanessa walks in.

"Vanessa . . ." I say, staring at her beautiful body.

"Dwayne's having another late night business meeting," she sarcastically says.

"Well, you know him better than I do."

"Jayson, I don't wanna be here with him."

"Then leave him," I say bluntly.

"I will, but I need your help," she pleads.

"Okay, I'll help you if I can, but if you're in this in any way with King, I can't protect you," I tell her.

"I'm not," she says as she steps farther into the room and looks out the window. "He usually doesn't show up until ten in the morning the next day," she says.

"Sounds like this is a routine."

"Yeah, it is. I'm his trophy girl. I'm to be seen but not heard. Everything a girl hopes to be when she grows up," she says with bitterness. "What about you, Jayson? Did you meet somebody special?"

"Yeah, I did. I married her and then she divorced me."

"Sorry about that. What about now? Is there someone in your life?"

"Well, not really. It's not what I want it to be right now." I wish I had met Mo'Nique under different circumstances.

"You know, since you've been here, I've been remembering what we had together. It brought back some feelings I didn't know I still had for you," Vanessa says. "I keep on thinking that this isn't the life I saw for myself when I was in high school. I thought I would be with you."

"Vanessa, I never forgot about you. We just had to do what was best for us back then."

"So what's best for us now?" she says as she turns to me and removes her white satin slip. The moonlight reflects off her perfectly sculpted body. Her firm breasts and large nipples are just as I remember them.

"Vanessa, we shouldn't . . ." But before I can finish my sentence, her lips are on mine. I feel like we're in high school again. She stands up in front of me and pulls down her panties. My dick gets hard looking at her neatly shaven triangle of pubic hair. She undoes my pants, pulls out my hard dick, and mounts me as I lie on the bed. She grabs my dick and rubs the head on her clit, making herself wet. The sensation is incredible, as I feel her warm juices on me. Then she pushes the head in her pussy, sliding the rest of me inside her.

Vanessa doesn't want to make love; she wants to fuck. She rides me like a jockey, bucking up and down. I can barely hold on as she grinds and bucks on my dick. Vanessa kisses me with passion as if she's been waiting to have me since the day she saw me again. I roll her over on her back, lift one leg, and stroke her wet pussy.

"Oh, shit . . . give it to me, Jayson!" Vanessa exclaims passionately.

Over and over, I pound her as she bucks back on my dick. I forgot how good her pussy felt. She bites her bottom lip and pinches her left nipple. I drop her leg and put my arms under her shoulders, giving it to her deep and hard, stroking into that wet vagina.

"I'm cumming . . ." Vanessa moans. "Ahhh . . . yes! Oh, Jayson, I want you to fuck me doggy-style like you used to."

I rise up off her. Vanessa gets up off the bed and turns around. I sit up on the edge of the mattress as she lowers her wet pussy around my dick, riding me again. Bending over, she touches the floor, bouncing her ass up and down, tightening her pussy around my dick. Then I stand behind her so I can hit it hard doggy-style while standing up. Damn, that ass is so fat and bouncy. Her cheeks jiggle as I hit it hard from the back, watching my wet dick go in and out of her. Vanessa's cum coats my throbbing member, letting me know that she's climaxed again.

After punishing her pussy for forty-five exhausting minutes, we both cum and collapse on the bed. I can't help but think that she fucks me more like a stripper than Mo'Nique does. The funny thing is, as good as the sex is with Vanessa, I still find myself wanting to be with Mo'Nique. After all these years of fantasizing about Vanessa, even while married to Lauren, it finally happens here of all places.

We lay on the bed in silence, breathing hard. After we both regain our composure, Vanessa puts her slip back on. "I still love you, Jayson," she says to me, then returns to her bedroom.

I didn't expect to hear her say that. Is she in love with Jayson Harper, the boy she knew in high school, or Jayson Harper, the undercover cop that's going to arrest her drug-dealing boyfriend? What do I really feel for Mo'Nique? Why am I thinking about her when I'm with Vanessa?

DAMIEN

"I had my doubts about Tommy, but he's a thoroughbred nigga," King says to me.

"That's what I told you, son. I didn't trust him either at first, but after he capped that nigga down in Atlanta for me, I had no doubt."

"Good, 'cause we gonna need a nigga like him down south running shit. Who are the other two new niggas you got down there?" he asks.

"Quan and Corey."

"Yeah, dem ma'fuckas and Horse will be able to help him run it," King says.

"So, let me ask you something, my nigga. Did you ever think we would be running shit like this?" I ask him. "You took down Bishop, the biggest gangsta in Harlem."

"I had no doubt about it. Bishop was a real OG, but he couldn't keep up with the times. And more importantly, he always used to underestimate me. Future King is what he used to jokingly call me. Well, he was right about that. You remember that night you saved my life back at that warehouse party in '93?" he asks.

"Yeah. That was a crazy night."

"I told you I got you for life. I meant that shit, my nigga," King says as he takes a drink. "I remember when I first saw you at Nard's house party back when you were a young gun. I saw that hunger in your eyes. I knew you were born to be a hustler, my nigga."

"I remember that night—a nigga was plotting on robbing you." We both laugh.

"Yeah, I know! That's why I had to get you on my team quick," King says as we laugh together.

King and I further reminisce about things at the club. I can't help but think about how he said Bishop used to underestimate him. Does King do the same thing with me? I owe King a lot—he's the one that got me in the game for real—but has he always had my best interests in mind? Or does he keep me close to make sure I ain't a threat to him? I guess that's some shit I've always asked myself but never tried to figure out.

That model bitch Charlene walks over to tell her Puerto Rican friend, Yaritza, about me. I hope she's down for some dick tonight.

As we knock back drinks, I see a nigga named Cornell on the dance floor. He used to hustle some shit for me three years ago. This ma'fucka stole ten grand and five bricks from me and skipped town. I've been dying to catch up with this ma'fucka. Last I heard, that nigga was in New Jersey, and then he disappeared. He must've heard I was down south and decided to come back in to town. Wrong night, nigga. I couldn't just run up on him in the club. Naw, I had to creep this nigga on some slick shit.

"Yo, King, you see that nigga on the dance floor in the FUBU sweater?"

"Yeah."

"That's the ma'fucka that stole those bricks and 10 grand from me," I tell him.

"Word? You gonna murda that fool?"

"Yeah, son. Yo, tell them girls I got some business to handle." I get up from the table and follow Cornell out to his car. He has a girl with him, so I let him get in his whip and follow him to a Holiday Inn down the road. This nigga goes and checks in and comes back and gets the girl, taking her to the room.

I follow him to the room and wait for them to get settled in. I wait about 15 minutes for that nigga to be getting busy with the girl he's with. I take out my .45 and creep to the door. I knock.

"Who is it?" he yells.

"Hotel security. Sir, do you own a black Honda Accord?" I ask through the door.

"Yeah," he answers.

"Somebody busted out your window, sir."

"What the fuck?" he yells as he comes rushing to the door and opens up. "I'ma fuck a nigga up!"

"Just what I was thinking, nigga," I say to him, pointing my .45 in his face.

"Oh, shit."

I buck him in the face and he falls on the ground, bleeding.

"Oh my God!" the naked girl in bed yells. This nigga is in his boxers trying to crawl away.

"Where ya going, nigga?"

"Shit, Dame! Dame! Listen!" Cornell yells.

"What, nigga?"

"I can explain."

"Explain what, nigga? How you thought you could rob me and get away with that shit?"

"I was gonna get right back with ya," Cornell yells.

"What? Fuck you, nigga!" I blast a nigga in the head.

The girl screams as Cornell lies bleeding on the floor. I turn and look at the bitch. "You ain't seen shit, right?" I say, pointing my gun at her.

"No! No, no!" she cries.

"Damn, ma, you looking all lovely and shit. Thick-ass thighs. Don't worry about it. This nigga was a punk anyway. I'ma call ya, though."

I walk out of the room, jump in the whip, and pull off. Honey was fine, but I'm glad I got that nigga. Have to show niggas that you can't take shit from me without consequences. Like Pac said, "Revenge is the sweetest joy next to getting pussy."

NIKKI

I can't believe Mo left Penny and me at the party the other night. I've been calling her cell, but she won't pick up. I dial her number from Penny's cell, and she finally answers.

"Hello," Mo'Nique says.

"Well, damn, you don't wanna talk to me now?"

"Nikki, I just need to take care of some things."

"So you can't call me back?" I say to her, pissed.

"Nikki, to be honest with you, I needed some space to get my mind right."

"Why? What did I do to you?"

"That whole shit at Trey-D's party really put things in perspective for me. I need to do something with my life."

"Oh God, why you trippin', girl? It was just a party, and I was making some extra cash."

"Nikki . . . I saw you and Penny freaking that dude upstairs. I can't get down with that anymore. If you wanna do that, go ahead, but I'm done."

"Mo'Nique, just because Tommy set you up at his house don't mean you better than us now!" I yell at her.

"No, I'm not better than you. I'm better than dancing for dumb niggas who just wanna use me," she says.

"So, what you gonna do? How you gonna make money then?" I ask her.

"I'm gonna get a part-time job and I'm going to night school."

"Oh, excuse me. Guess you don't need me no more."

"Nikki, I just need to get my life right. I don't got no problem with you. I love you. I just needed to do this for me."

"Okay, whatever, girl. I gotta go. Bye." I hang up, pissed.

That fool at the party paid Penny and me three grand to freak his ass. I wasn't gonna let that shit go. If she wants to be all uptight now, that's her problem. I can't believe how ungrateful that girl is! I took her ass in when she didn't have nowhere to live. Put her up on game. Just because she got Tommy in her life now she thinks she's the shit. Just wait till that nigga breaks her heart. They always do! Then her ass will come back here.

Why am I so concerned about what she does anyway? It's not like she's stopping my hustle. I almost feel jealous, but screw that. It's not like she's doing anything I want. I got these dumbass tricks to hustle. As a matter of fact, I'm getting ready to see Dre. It's been two weeks since Dre's cousin's funeral. Dre's been wanting to catch up with Damien and Horse. This is gonna turn into an all-out war. Luckily, Damien's been up in New York for a month now.

I go to The Pink Palace and make my money as usual, but I can't help but think about what Mo'Nique said to me. I can't really be mad at her. Lord knows in the past I thought about quitting this shit and doing something different, but I love making this money. I can't go back to minimum wages.

Dre comes into the club with two other dudes and they sit at a table in the back. I walk over to them.

"Hey, Dre."

"What's up, Nikki?" Dre says in a distressed tone.

I sit at the table. "How you doing?" I ask him.

"I just buried my cousin. What do you think?"

"I'm sorry, Dre."

"Yeah, so where's that New York nigga been at?" Dre says, pissed.

"Last I heard he went back up to New York," I tell him.

"So you don't know when he'll be back?"

"Not really. We ain't close like that. When he comes back is his business."

"He better stay where he at then, 'cause when dat nigga do, it's on," Dre says with a dreadful look on his face. "This nigga come into my town and start pushin' weight on my corners, messin' wit' my lady, and kill my cousin? We gonna show him how we do things down in the A, for sure," he promises.

"Since when am I your lady, Dre?" I ask him.

"You know you'll always be my lady."

Dre's partners get up and go sit closer to the stage.

"That's nice of you to say, Dre, but I don't want no man in my life," I tell him.

"You don't have to be my lady. I just wanna know can a nigga cut?"

"You know how that works, Dre," I say to him, rubbing my fingers together.

"That's cool wit' me, but I ain't talking about no VIP room, either."

"I think we can change that," I tell him.

We end up going back to his place in Bankhead and cuttin'. Dre's really in an exceptional form tonight. He works my ass in almost every position he can bend me. We're tearing down the walls in his room for about three hours before he finally wears himself out. Thank God for K-Y Jelly, or I'd be tore up, for real. It seems like Dre's taking his anger out on my pussy. I'm worried about what Damien would do to me if he finds out about Dre. I'm probably gonna stop doing him after tonight. These two niggas are gonna kill each other.

I have him drop me off at my place. Dre hits me off with $500. I don't care what Mo'Nique says; there ain't no money like trick money.

MO'NIQUE

I'm really sorry Nikki thinks I'm avoiding her, but I have to step off and do what I have to do. After the party that night, I got on the Internet and signed up to complete my GED.

The next day, I'm at a job fair at the Georgia Convention Center, and I see my old high school friend, Nadia. I walk up to her in the huge convention lobby.

"Nadia?"

"Janelle, what's up, girl?" Nadia says and gives me a hug.

"Just trying to find a j-o-b, that's all. You too?"

"No, girl, I work at Harland in the call center. I just drove my cousin, Shay, down here to fill out some applications."

"Why don't you get her a job where you work?"

"I did, but the little heifer didn't like being on the phone all day and started calling in all the time until they fired her ass," Nadia says and laughs. "But why don't you come down and try it?"

"Yeah, that's cool. They hiring now?"

"Hell, yeah! Come on, girl, let's get you down there. When you fill out your applications put my name down as your reference so I can get my hundred dollar bonus."

"Look at you trying to make some extra on the side! Nadia, I don't think I ever really thanked you and your mom for taking me in back then," I say.

"Girl, my momma loved you. I'm just sorry I couldn't do more to help you back then. You never did tell me why you left home, but I figured it had something to do with your stepdad."

"Something like that. Thank you for not pushing."

"So, what have you been doing with yourself since high school?" she asks.

"Well, you know . . . odd jobs here and there," I say, avoiding the fact that I shake my ass at The Pink Palace. But Nadia has always known the gossip on everybody in high school, so chances are she knows about my working there. Better I say it than have her bring it up. "And I used to dance at The Pink Palace."

"Oh, you did?" Nadia says, faking like she's shocked to hear that.

"Nadia, you already knew that, so don't act."

"Well, I did hear something like that from Shardae that was in our algebra class. Her brother, Rashad, said he saw you dancing up there."

"Well, the rumors were true."

"Girl, don't be ashamed of doing what you had to do to survive. A lot of these bitches out here be having two or three babies from different niggas, living off of child support and welfare. You don't got any kids, do you?" she asks me.

"Naw . . . not yet. Do you?"

"Yeah, I got a little girl," Nadia says and shows me her pictures.

"Damn, you had a baby?"

"Yep, me of all people. I don't even like other people's kids!" Nadia says and we both laugh.

We spend the rest of the day catching up with each other. I'm sorry I lost contact with her, but I won't let that happen again.

Nadia hooks me up with an interview at Harland. After I interviewed at the call center in Decatur, I get the job and they put me in a training class starting that Wednesday.

It's been weird working in an office for the first time. No half-naked girls walking around, no drunk niggas grabbing my ass. Just a clean and professional part-time job that's easy and that I can handle. It gives me plenty of time to study for the math and science test I have this Friday. I almost feel like I'm back in school.

Tommy calls me and tells me he's gonna be back in town next week and that he can't wait to see me. I can't wait to see him, either. I've never been so excited to see a man.

This past week has been refreshing for me, like I can really start my life over again. But you know as soon as you think things are all good, your past reminds you of where you came from.

I'm on break at the Harland building, sitting outside, eating a sandwich, when two guys stop and stare at me. I'm used to guys looking at me, but these fools are cheesing and snickering to each other. I don't know them, but I know they recognize me from The Pink Palace.

"Excuse me, miss?" one of the guys says. I pretend not to hear him. Then he walks up to the table.

"Hey, do I know you from somewhere?" he says.

"No, you don't," I respond.

"Damn, you fine. I'd like to see you sometime."

"Sorry, I got a man," I tell him.

"Come on, girl. I've seen you dancing at The Pink Palace before. You were the finest thing up in there. I just wanna get a little private dance."

"Listen, I don't dance anymore, so if you and your little friend wanna point and laugh at me, I'll be happy to report you to human resources."

"Damn, give a ho a job and she don't know how to act. You ain't dat fine." He gets up from the table.

"And you ain't fine at all, ya troll-looking nigga."

"Oh, it must be your ass, 'cause it sure ain't yo' face! Go on and pop, lock, and drop it for me," he says as the other guy cracks up. Here we go again.

"That's right, my ass. My fine red ass you had to pay to see 'cause that's the only way you could ever see it. So, when you're jacking off tonight, make sure you thinking about my soft ass that my man is hitting," I say to them and walk away. That felt good, telling that asshole off. I wish Tommy could have seen me. Damn, I miss him.

7

Indecent Proposals

JAYSON

Since my unexpected encounter with Vanessa the other night, I haven't been able to think straight. At this point I can't afford to be caught slipping, or I could end up with a bullet in my head.

I told Mo'Nique that I'd be coming back to Atlanta in two days and that I couldn't wait to see her. She says a lot has changed with her in the last month. She told me that I would be proud of her. I feel so guilty now that she's changing her life for a man that doesn't even exist.

Lieutenant McNiven calls me on my cell and says that he wants to meet with me as soon as I return to Atlanta. I tell him that King and Vanessa are also coming down with Damien and me. He hasn't told me when the deal is scheduled to go down, or how they plan on bringing the cocaine into the city, so I guess King is taking extra precaution to make sure nothing goes wrong.

Damien told us about the guy he killed the other night—some dude that used to hustle for him who stole some bricks and money. It's just another charge to add to the case when we bring him down. It seems like Damien has become more reckless since being back in New York.

Damien and King are close, but I can see Damien becoming tired of being number two. King's the brains behind the empire, and Damien's his homeboy from back in the day. Damien, however, is growing more ambitious as time goes by.

As far as I can see, Vanessa is telling the truth. She has nothing to do with King's operation. She's not exactly a captive prisoner of King's, either. She's well taken care of. She spends most of her days shopping or hanging with some girlfriends. She always has a driver to take her wherever and a bodyguard to protect her, but she says he won't let her go. I wouldn't either.

The district attorney in New York is only interested in bringing King down. This would be one of the biggest drug busts in state history.

The most they've ever been able to charge him with is money laundering—accusations which were thrown out of court for lack of evidence. King's covered his illegal dealings even better since they came after him. He knows the feds are watching him, and he's literally given the system the middle finger, saying, "You can't touch me."

Today, King brought us out to Rucker Park to watch a street ball tournament he throws for kids in Harlem. Rucker Park is the home of legends like Pee Wee Kirkland, who once led Rucker in scoring during the 1970 and 1971 season. He once signed a one-year contract with the Chicago Bulls, but because of drugs, he couldn't play. Pee Wee once scored 135 points in a semi-pro game and averaged seventy points per game in one season. To this day, NBA players still come and play at the park during the off season, and they better bring their A game, too. Street ballers here are known for schooling the NBA's best.

King does this annual event to look good in front of the community. He buys a truckload of Nike and Rocawear clothing and gives it away to the local kids. He says he loves the kids, but then he turns around and sells crack to them on the streets. This guy is a walking contradiction in every sense of the term. I can't help but wonder how many kids here look up to this nigga and wanna be like him when they grow up, because that's the reality of what we're talking about here. As soon as we take down King, there will be another nigga to take his place. The cycle won't stop.

"Foul that nigga!" King yells as his team is trailing by two points. "Dumb-ass ma'fuckas," he utters to himself.

"Calm down, baby," Vanessa says, rubbing his arm. It's hard to believe I was just fucking the hell out of her the other night, and now she's hanging on King's arm like a faithful wife.

"Take the charge!" King yells again.

"Yo, King, take Horton out and sub him with Campbell," I tell him.

"Why?" he asks.

"Because Campbell can back their man down in the paint, forcing the double team. Then he can kick it out to Sidwell, who can bury the three if you can free him up."

King looks at me then makes the call to substitute Horton for Campbell. "I hope you know what you talking about," King remarks.

"Trust me."

Just as I said, Campbell gets the double team and then passes it out to Sidwell, who hits the three at the buzzer.

"Yes!" King yells. "Real good call, Tommy."

"Sounds like you used to play ball in high school," Vanessa says to me, knowing I did. She was a cheerleader for the team.

"Yeah, I used to ball a little."

"Bet you had all the girls on your jock, huh?" King remarks.

"Naw, just one girl, and she never left my side." I stare at Vanessa. She looks away, trying not to show her feelings in front of King.

Later on that night, I'm on a flight back to Atlanta.

MO'NIQUE

Tommy calls me and tells me he should be here in about thirty minutes. I can't wait to see him. I got no idea how I'm going to feel when he gets here. I feel so excited inside that it's killing me. Maybe I shouldn't let all my feelings out. Tommy is still in the game, and anything can happen, although I get the feeling when I'm around him that he doesn't want to be doing the things he's doing.

We never really talk about the stuff he does with Damien. I don't wanna be getting all in his business. Maybe I should talk to him about it. I don't know. I don't care right now. All I want to do is be with him.

I straighten up the house and go to LongHorn to get a steak for him. It's the best I can do, seeing as I don't know how to cook. I don't want him to come home hungry to the aroma of Pine-Sol.

I wonder if Nikki is gonna do anything for Damien when he gets home? I doubt it. I hear a key push in the doorknob, and my heart skips a beat. The door opens, and I see Tommy standing there, looking so damn sexy.

"Hey, you," he says.

"Hey," I say as my heart continues to rush.

Tommy puts down his suitcase and walks in. We stare at each other for a moment, and then I walk over and kiss him. Our lips tug at each other, and our tongues reconnect. I feel myself getting so wet. I pull away slowly, resisting the urge to rip his clothes off and rape him.

"How was your flight?"

"It was good. Damn, you look good," Tommy remarks.

"Stop that. Are you hungry? I bought some food for you at LongHorn. I would have cooked you something, but I tend to burn shit. I figure you wouldn't want to eat something that tastes burnt . . ."

Tommy stops me from babbling. "Mo'Nique, I'm not hungry for that."

"Then what do you want?" I ask.

Tommy steps to me and puts his arms around me, kissing my lips again. He picks me up, and I wrap my legs around his waist as he carries me to the bedroom.

Tommy lays me down on the bed and unzips my pants, pulling them off. Then he stares at me in my shirt and baby blue thong.

"You've been all I can think about, Mo'Nique."

"I've been missing you too."

Tommy's hands caress my legs and then slide up my inner thighs. I close my eyes and let my floodgates flow freely. Tommy pulls off my thong, and I take off my shirt. Then Tommy submerges head-first between my legs and pops my oral cherry. Up until that moment, I had never gotten head before. Sure, I've given it, but I've never *received* it.

I don't know how to react to it at first. I'm thinking as he's rubbing his thick, soft tongue up and down my slit that it feels weird but not all that. Then slowly his tongue goes deeper inside me, moving from the top to the bottom, and I feel myself get even wetter. I close my eyes and start to move my hips back and forth to match his tempo. Tommy's tongue swirls around my walls and I grab the sheets.

"Ahhhh!" I moan.

Tommy then finds my clit, which has swollen up to look like a miniature pacifier. He sucks and nibbles on it. Then it hits me. My knees buckle and my back arches up as if I were possessed.

"Oh, shit! Shit!" I yell passionately as I climax and feel a surge of juices explode from my pussy.

"You like that?" Tommy asks.

I nod because I can't really form a syllable at that point. Tommy stands up and pulls down his pants. I decide that it's my turn. Tommy has stopped me from giving him head before, but tonight, that dick is all mine. I sit up and grab his dick.

"Mo'Nique, you don't have to do that."

"I want to," I say to him as I put it in my mouth. I slide my tongue up and down his huge dick.

"Ahhh . . ." Tommy gasps.

Then I make it moist, dribbling saliva all over his dick and bobbing my head up and down his shaft, gradually at first, then picking up my pace.

"Mo . . . Oh God . . ." Tommy moans as he places his hand on the back of my head to guide me. He's mine now.

Then I really put it on him. I suck him like a cherry Popsicle, tightening my lips around his dick, sucking harder and faster, enjoying his taste. My lips curl over his penis head, letting his dick slide deep into the back of my throat. I bring him to the edge, and then slide him out of my mouth.

"Oh, shit!" Tommy staggers back, blown away.

"Did you like that?" I ask him.

"Oh, yeah, yeah." Tommy comes forward. I widen my legs for him as he plunges his dick into my wet pussy. This is off the chain! Tommy pumps into me passionately, making my cum squirt out of me with every deep thrust.

"More! Give it to me harder, Tommy!" I yell, and Tommy complies with my wishes. He positions himself on his knees at an angle that allows him to bottom out my pussy with every stroke. The passion that's been building up between us for the past month has finally found a release.

I've never been so soaking wet with sex juices before. Both of us are drenched in a creamy white fluid that allows him to go deeper and thrust more rapidly into me. His balls slap against my ass, and I want more. Our arms wrap around each other, pulling his chest against my breasts.

"Fuck me, Tommy!" I yell, not wanting the spasm in my pussy to end. We are like crazed animals, all over each other. I've never enjoyed sex like this before.

Tommy pulls out of me and flips me over flat on my stomach, entering my pussy again, lazy-dog style. I close my legs, tightening my grip on his dick and letting Tommy pump me even deeper than before. I'm so relaxed that I allow my next orgasm to come.

"I . . . I . . . I love it," I stutter out. Then I feel Tommy explode a load of cum inside me, and we lay in that position, breathing hard.

"I guess you had a lot to get out of you?" I ask him.

"Yeah, I think I just did." We both laugh as Tommy wraps his hands around me.

We are lying in bed as Tommy eats the food I bought. He's feeding me too.

"Oh God, you are such a pig!" I say to Tommy.

"What? What did I do?" Tommy says as he takes another mouthful of steak, dripping A1 sauce on the sheets.

"I just washed these sheets."

"Mo'Nique, after what we just got done doing on these sheets, you're gonna have to wash them again."

"You're so nasty." I hit him with the pillow.

"So, tell me about these big changes you've made," Tommy says.

"Well, first of all, I'm not going to dance at The Pink Palace anymore."

"Really, what changed your mind?"

"You . . . and I just got to a point where I'm looking at my life and it's not what I want it to be," I tell him.

"I'm glad to hear that."

"Also, I'm taking classes to complete my GED, and I got a job."

"What, a job? What happened to not wanting to work at Taco Bell?" he asks.

"Well, at least I can be someone who you wouldn't be embarrassed to be seen with."

"Mo'Nique, I've never been embarrassed to be seen with you."

"Well, I'm tired of men staring at me and thinking that I'm a ho because I dance at a club. I mean, I've done things I'm not too proud of, but there's more to me than that."

Tommy takes my hand. "I've known that since the day I met you."

"Tommy, you're the first man to ever treat me like a lady. Listen, I know you're doing your thing hustling, but I care about you." Didn't I say I wasn't going to open up my heart to him?

"I care about you too."

"I know there are things you said you can't tell me, but no matter what it is, I wanna be with you," I confess.

"Mo'Nique . . ." Tommy gets a strange look on his face.

"Tommy, it's okay. You don't have to tell me anything right now, but I do wanna tell you something."

"What?"

"My name, my real name. When I started dancing, I didn't wanna use my first name, so I started to go by my middle name, Mo'Nique. My real name is Janelle Mo'Nique Taylor," I say. I've never told any guy my name before.

"Janelle . . . I like it. When the time's right, I will tell you everything. I just don't wanna put you in danger," Tommy says.

"Is it that serious?" I ask.

"Yeah."

I really wanna know what's going on with Tommy now, but I'll wait for him to tell me. Something tells me that whatever it is, it's going to be bad for both of us.

DAMIEN

I'm back in Atlanta with King, and I can't wait for this deal to go down so that I can get back to

New York. I didn't realize I missed being there so much. I miss my seed, and being here is really preventing me from being there for him.

Shit, my dad checked outta my life when I was two. It's funny how I didn't get to know him until I was a grown man, and he was the biggest OG in Harlem. They called him Bishop. My mom got herself hooked on heroin, so I started working the corners for King. Damn, Mom used to bring home any nigga that wanted some ass so she could buy her next hit. I don't want my son to have to come up like that.

He won't have to grow up in Grant Projects the way I did. On the corner in the dead of winter, hustling or robbing other niggas just to eat. There are some things a kid should never have to go through or see. Maybe that's the reason why I am the way I am today. Maybe my shit ain't together because of what I had to go through. No real father to show me how to be a man. Fuck it. Those are the cards life decided to give me, so I decided to cheat at the game a long time ago.

King and Vanessa are staying at the home in Buckhead he bought two years ago. Vanessa is a dime for sure. I guess that's why King wants to lock her down. I guess she reminds him of Nikia Jones from back in the day. Even though she's fine, he still fuck around on the side. Kinda like how Trina's the wifey and Nikki's the mistress.

Trina's the chick I've wanted to be with since the day I saw her come out of a bodega in Harlem. Honey wasn't paying me no mind, no matter how hard I tried to get at her. Talking about how she had a man. About a month later, Trina broke down and let me hit that ass one night. I made sure I got her pregnant. Some girls you just gotta trap.

When I get to the crib out in College Park, I call up my local lady, Nikki, and tell her to bring her ass over here. I don't know what it is, but there's something about her that gets me harder than a bitch. Well, I do know what it is about her. It's that ass.

I wanna get with her cousin Mo'Nique, too. I hooked my dawg Tommy up with her, but I still wanna hit that ass. Tommy's gonna have to learn to share that pussy. I bet she's a freak just like her cousin, and she got an onion. I mostly fuck with dark-skinned girls 'cause the blacker the berry, the sweeter the juice, but I'd love to see how sweet that red berry is too.

"What's up, ma?" Nikki comes through about an hour later dressed in some Apple Bottom jeans and a baby doll shirt. I really did miss fucking her tall, fine ass. I gotta admit that I'm hooked on that pussy like a dope fiend. She got a round ass like that chick Deelishus on *Flavor of Love*. Makes a nigga just wanna jump on it for real.

"Hey, baby, you have fun in New York?" she asks.

"Naw, just business. What you been doing since I've been gone?"

"Just doing my thing at The Pink Palace."

"Cool. I've been dreaming about you, ma."

"Really? What you been dreaming about?"

"Actually, it's been more like a fantasy," I admit.

"You know I can do anything you want, baby. Just let me know," Nikki says and rubs my dick. Damn, this bitch is so fucking sexy. I bet her momma was a stallion too. It must run in the family, that's probably why her cousin is so fine.

I wonder if I've been going about getting at Mo'Nique's ass the wrong way. Maybe I should try a new angle.

"Word? All right, ma, what about a three-some?"

"What, I'm not enough for you?"

"Yeah, but one more would make it that much more better," I say.

Nikki walks over to the bar and pours herself a drink. I just love to see that ass in motion.

"All right, but it's gonna cost ya. I can talk to some girls at the club."

"I don't want that Penny girl, either."

"Then who do you have in mind?" she asks as she walks over with her drink.

"What about Mo'Nique?"

Nikki puts her drink down and glares at me. "You know that's my cousin. I don't get down with family members. That's just nasty."

"So you can watch her dance but you can't get down with her?"

"Hell no!" Nikki snaps at me.

"Damn, ma, hook a nigga up," I say as I caress her ass.

"Listen, I can find a girl for us, but not her. Besides, she says she ain't in the game anymore."

"Really?"

"Yeah, she quit dancing and got a job at Harland. Ain't she with ya boy, Tommy, anyway?" she asks.

"I don't know. It was just a suggestion. Any girls you find, just let me see them first," I tell her and kiss her lips.

"All right, daddy."

Damn, I really wanted to fuck Nikki and Mo'Nique's ass at the same time. Not like I haven't already had a threesome before, but to get both of them naked at the same time would've been a dream come true. She thinks I really give a damn that that's her cousin? Keep it in the family! So she quit dancing. It doesn't matter. Once a ho, always a ho. I just gotta creep her ass on some slick shit.

8

Who Am I?

NIKKI

I can't believe Damien tried me on doing some freak shit with my own cousin. I know he wants to get with her, but to try me on some threesome shit is nasty. That's like me asking him to get down with Dre and me. I bet that would turn his stomach. I bet he would get sick to know he's eating some pussy that Dre had his dick up in last night. I kinda want to walk out of here when he says that to me. He's lucky he's got deep pockets—that and a long tongue. Damien knows how to eat some good pussy.

I lay on my back on his bed with my legs spread wide while Damien buries his face in me. I close my eyes and become lost in a euphoric bliss. His tongue licks my clit back and forth as

I feel his bottom lip rubbing in my pussy. My juices pour into his mouth as I place my hand on the back of his head, trying to push his whole tongue into me.

"Oh, shit, that's it. Don't stop," I moan out to Damien.

"Yeah, you like that, don't ya?"

"Yes . . . that's it, daddy," I say as I feel my muscles spasm in my pelvis and torso.

"That's it, come for daddy, ma," Damien says as he flicks his tongue rapidly up and down my clit.

"Oh, fuck! Yes! Ooooohhhhh . . . shit," I cry out as my orgasm overwhelms me. At least he's good at that.

I stay the night at his place and think about how much longer I'm gonna fuck this nigga. I heard him on the phone with King earlier tonight. It turns out King wants to go out with Damien and Tommy to discuss the business and wants them to bring us to the house. Just the opportunity I've been waiting for to get close to this King guy and hustle him.

I guess Mo'Nique will be there too. I haven't talked to her since that day on the phone. I really miss her but I ain't gonna stop doing what I've got to do.

The next day, Damien and I drive out to Buckhead to the same gated community where Trey-D had the house party two weeks ago. Go figure. We pull up to the house and see Tommy's Cadillac parked outside and we go in. This nigga King must have crazy dough. Damn, all this time messing with Damien's ass is going to be worth it.

I walk in and see King and Tommy. Damn, this nigga is fine. He looks like a slimmer version of Winky Wright, but I see on his arm some other chick. She's pretty, kinda upscale looking. Damn, this nigga has a bitch already. Most niggas in the game have a lady or two on the side, but this look like his main bitch. I hate competition.

I see Mo'Nique sitting on the couch with Tommy, and I don't know what to say to her. I guess I should say the obvious. "Hey, Mo, how ya doing, girl?"

"I'm good, Nikki."

"King, this is my lady, Nikki," Damien says.

"Nice to meet you, Nikki."

"The pleasure is all mine," I say to him.

"This is Vanessa," King says as he smiles at me. Yeah, I can tell that he likes what he sees. I can also see the hate in Vanessa's eyes as she looks me up and down.

"Hello," she says in a sarcastic tone. She knows exactly what I'm here for.

"Hey," I say back, not giving a shit.

"Gentlemen, let us step out by the pool area. Make yourself at home, ladies," King says.

Believe me, once I get this bitch out of here, I will.

I know this bitch's type already. She's a siditty ho. I bet she came up in a middle-class family, a real daddy's girl. She probably went to college and got a degree of some sort. What her father don't know is that his little ho's on the down low. The type of girl that always wants to have a roughneck nigga on her arm, which explains why she's with King.

I know a gold digger when I see one, 'cause I'm the best there is at digging a nigga's pocket out. Look at her standing there with her nose up, thinking she better than us. She can see it in my eyes that I'm here to take her man.

You better believe that, bitch.

JANELLE

Tommy got a call this morning from this King guy inviting us to his home. Tommy told me that he's Damien's business partner from New York. In other words, King's a big-time hustler whom Damien is hustling for. Tommy tells me I don't have to go with him, but I want to see first-hand what kind of guy Tommy's working for.

We get to the house out in Buckhead just five minutes before Damien and Nikki arrive. Tommy introduces me to King, and I can see by the way he's staring at me that he's just like Damien. King then introduces me to his girl, Vanessa. She's beautiful—not the type of woman I expect to see a man like King with. She gives me a weird look and then looks at Tommy oddly. The tension in the air's so thick you can cut it.

Then Nikki and Damien come in. Nikki and I haven't talked to each other since I told her I wasn't dancing anymore. I expect her to have an attitude toward me, but she doesn't at all. I can tell Nikki's eyeing King like a vulture, and so can Vanessa. Nikki, I guess, takes away some of the glares that I'm receiving from Vanessa. I don't know if she's just insecure or what. I know some girls don't like it when new women come around their man, but I ain't even checking for King. It's Nikki she'd better be worried about.

"So, Mo'Nique. That's an interesting name. How did you meet Tommy?" Vanessa asks.

"Nikki actually hooked us up."

"Really, and what is it that you do, Nikki?" Vanessa asks her sarcastically.

"I dance," Nikki bluntly says. Nikki doesn't back down to no chick.

"Dancing? Hmm, do you dance too, Mo'Nique?" Vanessa asks.

"Not anymore."

"Oh, I see now why Tommy would be interested in you," Vanessa remarks condescendingly. What the fuck is her problem?

Vanessa sits on the couch and takes a sip of her drink. Nikki and me look at each other and roll our eyes.

"Anyway, how's school, Mo?" Nikki asks.

"It's coming along. I should be able to test out in two months," I tell her.

"You're in college?" Vanessa asks.

"No, not yet."

"How old are you?" Vanessa asks.

"I'm twenty."

"So, you're going to school for your GED? Wow, so what's next for you, a community college?" Vanessa rudely asks.

Okay, that's enough. I don't gotta take this shit from no uppity, gangsta ho. "If that's what I choose to do, yeah. So, what is that you do?" I ask her, pissed off.

"I got a bachelor's degree in business management. I graduated from NYU," Vanessa says.

"And you're doing what with your bachelor's?" I ask.

"I don't have to work," Vanessa contentedly says.

"So, in other words, you an educated gold digger," Nikki snaps sarcastically. Leave it to Nikki to call a bitch out on her shit.

Vanessa rolls her eyes and gets up with her drink. "I don't have to deal with some broke-ass strippers," Vanessa says as she walks out of the room.

"What? Fuck you, too, you whack-ass weave beyotch."

I hold Nikki back before she grabs that bitch by her extensions.

"Girl, she don't know me. I will wipe her stank ass in her own home," Nikki says.

"I know you will. Don't even trip about that ho. If she thinks she's all that because she's screwing a drug dealer, then let her."

"Shit, she better watch her back before I take her man," Nikki says.

"Nikki, I don't think you should be playing games with these niggas. Damien ain't the most stable-minded guy around. These New York guys are straight killers," I remind her.

"Girl, I'll be fine. I got Damien wrapped around my clit like a baby. So, how are things with you and Tommy?" Nikki asks.

"Nikki, I know you think that I'm being stupid for falling for him, but I can't help it. We just have this connection. I can't explain it."

Nikki looks at me and then puts her hand on my shoulder. "Mo, I'm sorry for coming down on you the way I did the other day. If you really have feelings for Tommy then I ain't going to hate on that. I just don't wanna see you get hurt, especially after what you've been through," Nikki says.

"Thank you. I really do love you, Nikki. I can't thank you enough for all you've done for me."

"Shut up. You gonna make me cry and mess up my mascara. You know I gotta be on point."

I laugh and we sit on the couch and catch up with each other. An hour later, we see the guys walk back in, and Vanessa is with King.

"So, we gonna break out, all right?" Tommy says to King.

"All right, my nigga."

"Good night, Tommy," Vanessa says and gives Tommy a look that a woman with strong feelings would give a man.

"You guys have a good night too." Tommy looks away, trying not to be too noticeable about it.

She's flirting with Tommy. That was definitely more than a "see you later." Is that why she's coming at me like that? What the hell is going on? Is this what Tommy's not telling me?

JAYSON

As we drive back on Peachtree Street, I notice how quiet and distant Janelle is. I'm nervous enough as it is, bringing Janelle around Vanessa. There's no telling what she could have said to her. Judging by the expression on Janelle's face, something bad happened. I guess I should just go ahead and set the bomb off now.

"What's on your mind?"

"Nothing," Janelle says, annoyed at something.

"Come on, Janelle. You've had this look on your face since we left the house. What's going on?"

"That's what I'm trying to figure out, Tommy. What is going on?"

"What?"

"Vanessa. I saw the way you two were looking at each other, and don't tell me I didn't see it."

"Janelle, it's more complicated than you think."

"Then uncomplicate it for me," Janelle says.

Damn, if I lie again, it'll only make shit even more stressful for her.

"I knew her from high school."

"Oh my God, you two were together back then?" I don't answer her. "Why didn't you say something to me?"

"Janelle, what was I going to say to you? That twelve years ago I was with a girl who's now with a major hustler?"

"Tommy, if King finds out, do you know what he'll do?"

"Yeah, I think I know," I tell her.

"No wonder she was coming at me like that." Janelle stares out the window. She then turns and looks at me. "When you were in New York, did you sleep with her?"

I look at her and then turn away. It starts to rain lightly outside.

"Wow, complete silence. I guess that answers that question. Pull over," Janelle demands.

"What?"

"I said pull over. I'm getting out."

"And go where? It's raining," I say.

"Either pull the fucking car over or I'll jump out!" she yells.

"Fine."

I pull over to the curb and Janelle gets out, slamming the door. She starts to walk down the sidewalk in the rain. I turn off the engine, get out, and start to follow her.

"Janelle, Janelle! Wait up!" I yell.

"For what, Tommy?" Janelle starts to cry. I catch up with her and grab her arm. She pulls away.

"Will you let me explain?"

"Explain what, Tommy? You never explain shit to me! You have all your little secrets that you won't tell me! I can't believe I thought that you could be honest with me! Nikki was right. I was stupid to believe you could ever love me. All I am to you is some stripper that you're fucking right now," Janelle says.

"That's not true. You mean more to me than that."

"No matter how much I change my life, it won't change who I am, or what I was. You can't be real with me because I don't mean nothing to you."

"It's not that simple!"

"It is, Tommy! If you really care about me, it is." Janelle stares into my eyes with tears in her eyes. "Just what I thought." Janelle turns around and walks away.

"I'm a cop."

I can't believe I just said that. What the hell am I thinking? I just blew my cover.

Janelle turns and looks at me in shock. "You're a cop?"

I stare in her eyes.

"My name is Officer Jayson Harper. I've been deep in cover in Atlanta for five months. That's my secret. I never meant to feel . . . I didn't know I would feel like this for you. I never meant to lie to you," I say to her as she stares into my eyes in disbelief.

"I knew there was something different about you, but not this. Now it all makes sense. Were you ever going to tell me?" she asks.

"Yeah."

Janelle stares at me and then closes her eyes. "Vanessa knows who you are. If she says something to King, you're dead."

"Vanessa wants out. She's not going to say anything to him. She's counting on me bringing him down," I tell her.

"She's counting on you? Do you still love her?"

Damn, I wasn't expecting her to just come right out and hit me with that question.

"I did. . . . I thought I still did, but I don't feel the same way about her like I feel for you. I love you."

A tear falls from Janelle's eye. "I don't know you," she says and walks away.

She's right. I don't even know myself anymore. I just compromised my cover and possibly
my life for a woman I barely know. I've got a job
to do, and all I seem to care about is her. Who
the hell am I anymore?

9

One Way or Another

DAMIEN

Back on the corner, we set up shop just like we did up north. We get these bitches with houses, move in, pay their rent, and cook the coke. We sell the shit right there. The problem is, some of these bitches get a little too greedy. Sure, we hit them off with a supply of whatever it is they're using, but some just can't get enough.

For instance, take this bitch, Yvonne. We set up in her house three months ago. We did our usual thing and hit her off with some blow. Turns out her man Curtis is a fiend, too, and they decide to have a private party with my shit.

Tommy and I are driving down Riverdale Road when we see these fools coming out of a QT gas station.

"Yo, Tommy, there's that bitch Yvonne and her man Curtis." I pull into the parking lot in front of them and we jump out. Yvonne and Curtis start to run, and I catch her ass behind the building.

"Where you running to, bitch?" I yell.

"Damien, please!" she yells.

I slap her and she falls on the ground. "I want my money, bitch!" I pull her hair and put my .45 in her face.

"Anything you want, Damien! Please, don't kill me!" Yvonne yells.

"You got one week, bitch. I want my fucking money!" I shove her on the ground.

I turn and see that Tommy is caught up with Curtis's bitch-ass. Curtis tries to fight Tommy and punches him in the face. Tommy then proceeds to kick the shit outta that nigga. I don't know what's gotten into Tommy, but he's stomping this nigga like a cockroach. He's been real irritable this past week.

"Who the fuck you trying, nigga?" Tommy yells. "Bitch-ass mutherfucka!" Tommy kicks him in the face. I see a nigga that works in the QT on his cell phone calling the cops, and I grab Tommy.

"Come on, nigga. We gotta go," I say.

"Fuck that shit! This nigga think I'm playing with him!" Tommy still wants to beat this nigga's ass.

"Tommy, come on, man!" I pull him off of Curtis and we hop back in the car and take off.

I've never seen Tommy so fired up. Usually, it's him telling me to calm down, but something has got him pissed.

"Yo, what's up with you, Tommy?" I ask him as we turn back on to Riverdale Road.

"Nothing."

"You were kicking homeboy to sleep back there."

"That nigga punched me," Tommy says.

"Yeah, but you been acting funny all week, nigga. What's going on?"

"Nothing, man, just some bullshit."

"Mo'Nique ain't taking care of you?" I ask.

"Fuck her, man," Tommy says.

"What? I know you fucking her. What's wrong? She ain't break you off right, son?" I say with a laugh.

"She ain't nothing, man. Plenty more ass in Atlanta," Tommy remarks and then spits out the window.

"That's what I always say to you, nigga. Too many hoes out here to be tied down to one." He just told me what I wanted to hear him say.

Yeah, plenty of ass, nigga, and soon I'm gonna be getting up in Mo'Nique's.

***

That night, I go by Nikki's house at about one o'clock in the morning. I know Nikki and Penny are at The Pink Palace. Since Mo'Nique's stopped dancing, I know she'll be there by herself. I knock on the door and she answers.

"Who is it?" Mo'Nique asks.

"It's me, Damien."

She opens the door for me and she's dressed in a T-shirt and shorts. Damn, her thick ass is fine. "Nikki's at the club tonight, Dame," she says.

"I know. I wanted to talk to you."

"About what?"

"About Tommy," I say.

She gets a sad look on her face, then lets me in. "What about Tommy?" she asks.

"What happened between you two? You got my man all stressed."

"I didn't do anything to Tommy. Whatever he's going through, that's on him," Mo'Nique says as she leans against the wall. I can't help but stare at her smooth, thick thighs.

"All right. I just wanted to know what's up. So, how you doing?"

"I'm fine, Damien. Look, it's late and I gotta get up early tomorrow for work," she says.

"So, you quit dancing? That's cool. A girl like you is too fine to be shaking ass at a strip club."

"Thanks. Is that all?"

I walk up to her and put my hand on the wall next to her.

"I just wanna know if there's anything I can do for you."

"Damien, I told you that I ain't messing with you. You're with Nikki, and I don't do shit like that to my family."

"Come on, ma. You know what I can do for you. I just wanna know if you can do all the shit Tommy says you can do," I say to her as I caress her leg.

She pulls away. "I don't give a shit what Tommy said to you! And I don't need anything from you," Mo'Nique says.

She thinks this is a game, so I grab her arm and pull her close to me. I press my dick up against her leg. "I ain't playing with you, Mo'Nique! You know how I get down. Just relax and let's have some fun." My dick gets harder, pressing up on her.

"Or what? You gonna rape me? I don't think Tommy's gonna like that."

I kiss her lips and rub her soft titty. She turns her head. I'm gonna just take this pussy right here. I don't give a fuck. This bitch is too fine.

"Tommy don't give a shit about you. Now you can give me that ass or I can take it."

Mo'Nique nods her head and pulls off her shirt. Her titties are prettier up close than they look on stage. I grab her left tit and put it in my mouth and start to suck it. I push my hands in her shorts, and she clenches her legs together. I grab her by the neck and push her head up against the wall.

"Don't fight me, bitch!"

I can see the fear in her eyes. She knows I mean business. She opens her legs. Just as I get my hand under her panties, a car pulls up in the driveway. Shit, it's Nikki and Penny's ass. I pull up off of her.

"Put your shirt back on. Don't say anything or you know what will happen to Nikki and you."

"Okay."

I sit on the couch and turn on the TV as Nikki and Penny walk in the door.

"Hey, what are you doing here, baby?" Nikki asks me.

"What do you think? Waiting for you, ma. I just got here a minute ago and decided to make myself at home and wait for ya," I say.

Nikki looks at Mo'Nique, and I know she thinks that I'm lying, but she doesn't say anything about it to me.

"Oh, okay. Come on, daddy. I don't wanna keep you waiting anymore. Good night, Mo."

Mo'Nique just nods her head to her. I give her a look before I walk into Nikki's bedroom behind her. She knows I'm going to get her ass one way or another. It's just a matter of time.

MO'NIQUE

He tried to rape me. That dirty muthafucka would've raped me in the living room. I was so scared. It felt like I was 16 years old again, helpless as James raped me. It's going to happen again. I can't stop him. Thank God Nikki and Penny came home when they did. Damien is fucking crazy—he would've killed me. I'm just a piece of ass to him, something less than a woman. A ho. I can't even tell Tommy what happened.

He's a cop. Tommy's a cop. That's not even his real name. He's been lying to me since the night we met. I should just wipe my tears away and forget him. I completely opened myself up to him, and he lied to me. He fucked that bitch Vanessa! I hate him. I hate him and Damien.

Stop fucking crying! You don't give a shit about no trick! That's all he is, that's all he ever was! You're a hustler, Mo'Nique, shake it off.

I just fooled myself into thinking I felt something for him. Fucking pig! I should have told them who he was, but I couldn't do it. I don't want them to kill him, and that pisses me off even more, that I still care about him.

I hate Jayson so much. So why am I at his door? I drove here as soon as Damien went in the room with Nikki. I couldn't stay there tonight. Not with him there. I just got in my car and drove to Jayson's place. He's the last person I want to see, but I need him. I got nobody else to turn to. But he doesn't care about me. . . . I shouldn't have come here. He's just a cop doing his job.

Just as I turn and start to walk back to my car, the door opens.

"Janelle?"

As soon as I hear his voice, I feel my eyes water up. He walks outside, and I can't move. He lied to me. I shouldn't be here, but as soon as he touches my back, I can't hold it back anymore, and I start to cry.

"Janelle, what's wrong? What happened?" Jayson asks.

I can't talk. I just break down in his arms and cry. Jayson wraps his arms around me, and I feel safe again. How can somebody that hurt me so bad make me feel so good? Jayson takes me inside and we sit on his sofa.

"What happened, Janelle?"

"If I tell you, you're going to do something stupid and get yourself killed."

"What? What happened? Tell me, baby."

"Damien . . . tried to rape me tonight."

Jayson doesn't say a word. He just gets up, goes in his room, and comes out three seconds later with his gun. I jump up off the sofa and grab Jayson.

"No! Jayson, don't do this, please," I beg him.

"He's dead! This ends tonight!" Jayson yells.

"Please, baby, don't do this. You can't. Please."

Jayson looks in my eyes, and I gently take his gun out of his hands.

"Did he hurt you?"

"No . . . he would've if I didn't let him. Nikki and Penny came home before he could do anything to me."

"Tomorrow you're going to pack a few bags and you're going to come and stay here with me," Jayson tells me.

"But what about Damien? He's going to know I said something to you."

"Just leave Damien to me. I'm not going to let him hurt you," Jayson says as he caresses my face. "Do you forgive me?" he asks.

"Yeah. I understand the situation you were in, Tom— Jayson. It was just hard to know you slept with her."

"I'm sorry. I didn't expect to see Vanessa again. I didn't know I would have feelings for you. I didn't even know what we really had."

"So, you do love me?" I ask him.

Jayson looks at me. "Yeah, I do." He kisses me.

"It's just going to be weird calling you Jayson now."

"How about I call you Janelle when we're here?" Jayson suggests.

"Okay."

"Are you sure you're okay?"

"Yeah, I was just scared. Can you just hold me tonight?"

Jayson smiles and takes me to his bedroom. He undresses me and we lie in bed together. Jayson holds me. It doesn't matter to me if his name is Tommy or Jayson. I just know that when I'm with him, I feel loved and safe. I don't wanna let him go.

Later that night, we talk about Jayson's life for a change.

"So, where are you from?" I ask him.

"Savannah. I went undercover here five months ago."

"How long have you been an undercover cop?"

"Four years."

"So, is that why your wife left you?" I ask.

"Yeah, Lauren and me were married for one year before I got assigned to the undercover unit in Atlanta. She couldn't handle me doing this. I don't blame her."

"I know how she feels. For this past week, I kept on expecting to open the paper and see 'Undercover Cop Found Dead in Some Alley.' Jayson, Damien is a psycho. He's going to know something's wrong."

"I've been getting close to Damien for five months now. He thinks I'm a hustler from Chicago. No one has ever been this deep, and as soon as King puts this deal together, we're going to bring them all down," Jayson reveals.

"I hope it's as simple as you say it is. What happens to us after that?"

"I've been thinking that. After this assignment, I was going to transfer to a different department down in St. Pete."

"St. Petersburg? What's there?" I ask.

"I got family down there. It's quieter down there. Maybe you could come with me."

"I don't care where we go, as long as I'm with you."

Jayson kisses my lips, and I wanna believe everything will be fine just as he said, but I know my life ain't a fairytale. Happy endings only happen in bedtime stories. I will hold on to Jayson as long as I can and try to avoid facing the inevitable.

10

Hot Shot

JAYSON

Damien's lucky that I'm a cop, or I would've killed his ass last night. I know he wants to get with Janelle, but I didn't think he would go this far. I shouldn't be surprised. This nigga is grimy enough to do anything. Janelle has been through enough bullshit in her life, and I can't put her in danger anymore. It's bad enough having Vanessa being so close to King and worrying about her safety as well. How did this all become so damn complicated?

It feels so good waking up with Janelle lying naked in my arms. I didn't think she would ever forgive me for lying to her. I thought I fucked up what we had like I did with Lauren. Somebody up there must like me.

"Janelle . . ."

She smiles when I call her that. "It feels so good to hear you say that to me."

"It feels good to say it. I was thinking that you should leave town until I wrap this up."

"But I thought I was going to stay here with you."

"It's too dangerous. Whenever you're here or at Nikki's house, Damien can still get at you."

"Where would I go?" she asks.

"To Savannah, until I take care of this. As soon as it's done, we'll go to Florida."

"I don't wanna leave you here, Jayson. What if something happens?"

"I'll be able to take care of myself, but I can't do my job if I'm worried about you. Trust me."

"I do," Janelle says, and I kiss her forehead.

"Good, so we're going to go to Nikki's house, then we're gonna pack you a bag and get you to Savannah."

"Okay. I love you, Jayson, so you better not get yourself killed," Janelle says to me.

"I promise." I kiss her lips.

She parts her thighs, and I penetrate her wet walls, sliding deep inside of her. This is heaven. Her body is so soft, and her lips are so moist.

We make love for hours as if it's our first and last time together. I feel my muscles tighten and her pussy clenches my dick as I explode between her legs. I bury my dick deeper inside her and let my cum gush into her warm pussy. We both climax together, and I know I can't lose her. I haven't felt this way about a woman for a long time.

We drive to Nikki's house, Janelle packs her bags, and we leave.

"Take care of yourself, Jayson."

"Call me as soon as you get into town."

"I will." We kiss again. She gets in her car and drives away. At least I know she's safe now, and I can deal with Damien.

I pick up Quan, and we go to a restaurant to get a meal. King and Damien treat Quan, Corey, and Horse like shit. He maybe hits them off with $1,000 a month, and they do all the dirty work. They take all the risk and get none of the big money that flows in day after day. When he can, Quan sends his mom in Brooklyn half of what he makes. This kid is too smart to be played like this.

"So, Quan, how did you get down with Damien in the first place?"

"I was running the streets, selling dime bags, and Damien saw me. He gave me ten small, folded-up pieces of aluminum foil with heroin in them and told me if I could sell it by the next day, he would put me down with the Flip Set and take care of me."

"Let me ask you something. Is he really taking care of you?"

Quan takes a bite of his burger and swallows it. "I could be doing worse."

"Or you could be doing better."

"Yo, Tommy, if I could, man, I wouldn't be here doing this shit. I would be doing like you said—I'd be in college. I was born an underdog in American society. If I was born in Beverly Hills with the right skin tone, I'd be good, but I was born with the have-nots. I just wanna take care of my mom and little sister. I don't wanna see her swinging around a pole, dancing to make a dollar."

"I understand ya."

"Believe me, Tommy, if I could be in school, taking care of them, I would."

I wish I could help him get out of this before it all comes crashing down around him. Quan is a good kid in the wrong business. Maybe I can help him cut a deal. It's times like these I feel like a sellout.

One hour later, I meet up with King and Damien at King's place up in Buckhead. Vanessa has gone out shopping for the day. That's a good thing. Now I can just focus on working these niggas over. I wanna just blast Damien in the face, but I got a job to do first. I know this nigga's foul, but to do something like that to Janelle just makes me wanna take him down even more. All these months of deep cover have been building up to this deal. No wires, no taps and no back-up is how we've had to play it to get King out in the open like this.

"Tommy, my connection from L.A. is coming into town Saturday night. They bringing enough snow to make it cold in July. That's the reason I sent Damien down here to set shit up. It'll make shit easy for us when this happens. When this goes down, we're gonna have Atlanta on lock," King says.

"Damn right. Where is it going down, so we can have niggas in place just in case things get shady?" I ask him.

"When the time's right, you'll know all you need to know. So for now, just relax and stay on point."

"What about security?"

"I got that under control. We just can't have any fuckups on our part. That's where you come in," Damien says to me.

"Me . . . what you talking about?" I ask him.

"I see the way you handle Quan and Corey, and we gonna need niggas like you making sure them young niggas stay focused. We gonna get this money," he says.

"A'ight, my nigga. You know how I do." *You just don't know how focused I am, nigga. I'm gonna lock your ass down in Rikers again, mutherfucka.*

NIKKI

When I get up this morning, or should I say this afternoon, I see a letter from Mo'Nique on the table. I open it. It reads:

> *Hey Nikki,*
>
> *I hate to take off like this, but I had an emergency. I had to leave and take care of Aunt Gene in Valdosta. I'll call you when I get there. Take care of yourself.*

Auntie Gene? We haven't seen her for years. I didn't even know Mo still kept in contact with her. Well, I guess somebody gotta look out for the family.

Damien came through with no warning last night. I'm not sure I like that. He says I'm his lady and shit, but then he leaves for a month and doesn't call. He knows I'm a stripper, but he doesn't care as long as I'm there for him whenever he calls. I know he fucks with other girls, so how can he think that I don't mess with other men? It's like we have these unspoken rules that we play by. This ain't a love thing, and he knows that as long as he gives me cash, he can get some ass.

Despite our weird relationship, we still take mini vacations together. One weekend, we went to Miami's South Beach and partied on the yacht he rented. Other times, he treats me to shopping sprees at the Lenox Mall.

I've never messed with a trick with this kind of money before, and I don't think he's ever fucked with a girl that looks like me. Sure, he's had other pretty women, but I'm his own personal fantasy chick or something. Plus, sexually, I've done things to Damien no other woman has. That's why he's addicted to my pussy.

Damien left $1,000 for me to spend, so I head straight to Lenox Mall and into Macy's to get some of Beyoncé's House Of Deréon fashions. I gotta step my game up if I plan on taking King away from Vanessa's stuck-up ass. Not like she's that much competition for me. She's a pretty girl, but I am the shit. I'm like a cross between Naomi Campbell and Meagan Good, with an ass that can stop traffic. That's why I'm the top seed moneymaker at The Pink Palace. I coulda been a model if things were different. Most bitches that dance in the club look like dogs, but Mo'Nique and me, we're like supermodels up in there. Not hoes with bullet holes and cigarette burns.

On my way out of Lenox Mall, I run into Dre and some of his niggas in the parking lot.

"What's up, Nikki?" Dre says.

I walk up to the car and bend over, putting my head in the window. I can see the way Dre's boys stare at my fat, round ass, and I love it.

"What's up, Dre? Where are you off to?"

"We're heading down to College Park to handle some business."

I look in between the seats and I see a Mac-11 semi-automatic submachine gun half exposed, and I know what business he's gonna handle.

"I heard that New York nigga was back in town, so we gonna show him what time it is."

Shit, this is not what I wanna see go down. Dre's gonna go and try to kill Damien's ass for what he did to his cousin. I say *try* because Damien isn't just another corner boy Dre can just roll up on. Damien has a small army down in College Park ready to ride, and a part of me doesn't wanna see Dre dead in the streets like his cousin Rodney.

"Dre, you can't just ride down there and go at Damien like that. He's got people looking out for you. As soon as you get there, he'll be waiting for you," I tell him.

"I don't give a fuck who he got looking out for him. They can get it too!" Dre exclaims.

Dre's dead serious about killing Damien, and I know the only thing that can stop him. I know his one weakness, and that's me. Since Dre was seventeen he's been in love with me. Anything I want, he'll do it for me, so I decide to run interference for Damien.

"I know you gonna ride on them, but wouldn't it be better to do it when Damien's actually in town?" I lie.

"In town? Where the fuck is he?" Dre asked.

"Damien went down to Miami last night."

"Shit! When that nigga coming back?"

"He didn't say, but since you don't seem to have anything to do tonight, why not spend it with me?" I say to him and rub my hand down his chest.

Dre smiles and gets that same lustful look in his eye again. But Dre's no fool. "Why you wanna kick it with me tonight?" he asks me suspiciously.

"I've been thinking about you a lot lately, Dre, and after the way you put it on me the last time we hooked up, you've been all I been wanting to do."

It wasn't really that much of a lie. Sure, I was playing a dangerous game with his emotions, but I did teach him everything he knows about fucking. Dre was very green on how to sex a woman right back in the day. Like most boys, Dre only knew how to catch a nut real quick. Up until me, he'd only fucked with young girls who didn't know shit about how to make a man extend his orgasm and make a bitch catch her nut first. I turned his young ass out by doing shit to him no other woman did. I'm the one that taught him how to eat pussy so good and introduced him to the Ghetto Kama Sutra. I was basically the Yoda to his Skywalker. The other night, he really showed me how much he had learned.

We end up heading to a nearby Days Inn and picking up where we left off the other night. The sex is erotic and raunchy. I have to admit that I do enjoy fucking Dre again. At first, when we hooked up in The Pink Palace, it was just a quickie. I was just trying to get him off and get paid, but these last two times we've hooked up, Dre was really trying to get me off for a change.

"That's it, Dre. Don't stop," I say as Dre pounds his dick deep into my pussy.

"You like that, Nikki?"

"Ahhh, shit, yeah, daddy. Keep it right there," I say as I dig my nails into his back.

Dre digs deeper into my gushy pussy and blows my back out with his powerful thrusts. It feels so good that I close my eyes and release my cum all over his dick. Dre continues to pump away, until his dick finally explodes with cum.

He collapses on top of me. Our bodies intertwine as we lay huffing and puffing, enjoying the sensation of our orgasms. Dre just fucked me better than Damien ever has. Dre rolls off of me and lies on the bed with his dick still fully hard.

"That was good as hell, Nikki," Dre says to me as he catches his breath.

"You still the shit, Dre. You be making me feel like how a woman should feel."

"I keep on telling you that, but you keep on fucking with that whack-ass New York nigga. I know you all about the dollar, Nikki, but that nigga can't treat you the way I treat you."

"Dre, we go back. That's why I mess with you still, but I ain't trying to be tied down."

"So what do you think that New York nigga is doing to you?" he asks.

"Damien thinks what I want him to. As long as he breaks me off, it'll stay that way."

"Is that why you lied to get me here? 'Cause you know one way or another I'm gonna kill his ass?" Dre says. Shit, Dre's smarter than I give him credit for.

"So, if you knew I was lying to you, why did you come here with me?"

"Because I really do care about you, Nikki, and I wanna be with you. I know you better than you think. You're a hustler just like me, and that's why I love you. I'm gonna put myself in the position where you won't have to dance at the club or fuck with no other niggas. You just wait and see. Pretty soon I'll be running this shit."

For the first time ever, I believe Dre plans on doing everything he says. I've never heard so much conviction in his voice before. Maybe he does know me better than I thought, and that turns me on. Perhaps that's the reason I've always fucked with Dre, because we're so similar, like two peas in a pod.

I grab Dre's hard dick and start to jack him off. I get up on him and slide his dick back inside of me and ride the shit outta him. I don't know if it's his ambition, his feelings for me, or that big dick of his—maybe all three—but for once I really wanna be with Dre.

***

DAMIEN

I've become more like King during my stay in Atlanta, and I don't know if that's a good or bad thing. I'm getting used to the idea of lying back and calling the shots instead of getting my hands dirty. Letting Corey, Quan, and Horse run the spots does have its appeal, but I miss the action for some reason. Horse is right about the corners down here being hot. These fiends come through like clockwork. It's a good thing we got these local cats down here helping the fiends get their fix.

I've snorted some dope in the past, but I've never let myself get hooked on that shit. I only fuck with X when I really wanna get my freak on with a bitch. Did that shit with Nikki once, and we were fucking off the walls. I wonder what Mo'Nique would be like if I did that with her.

Nikki and Penny fucked shit up with her the other night. I was gonna fuck the shit outta that red bitch. Even though Nikki messed things up, I still had a good time fucking her ass. You know how it is when you've been hitting the same bitch for a while. It gets boring. With Nikki, it's like a different porn flick every time.

I haven't seen Mo'Nique since the other night. I'm gonna have to see what's up with her soon.

Tommy seems more focused now than he did a few days ago. I guess with this deal about to go down, Tommy knows things are gonna change. He just don't got any idea how much I'm gonna change the game. I've been a soldier in King's army for too long. It's time to become my own general. I've studied this game for too long not to be a major player in it.

King thinks he's smarter than me. He thinks he can hit me off with pocket change like Corey and Quan while he makes millions. The street value alone of the cocaine we cook is about fifteen to twenty grand per kilo. At a street price of around $100 per gram, the actual street value of a single kilo can quickly escalate to $189,000. Six kilos of coke could ultimately sell for $1.1 million on the street, and the fact that I'm only making $100,000 off of that shit is crazy!

King is paying these ma'fuckers out of L.A. ten million cash for the hook-up they about to supply him with. That shit's gonna triple on the streets, and all I get is a 10 percent raise out of it? I think it's time to renegotiate my contract. King has been my nigga for a long time now,

The Pink Palace

and I've had his back since day one, and this is how he thanks me? I'm a loyal nigga, but if you fuck me over, then I got no choice but to fuck you.

I'm chilling at my house in College Park when Horse hits me on the Sidekick.

"Yo, what's up, nigga?"

"What up, son? Yo, I got something to tell you," Horse says.

"What is it?"

"Yo, you know how you told me to keep an eye on that Dre nigga?"

"Yeah."

"Well, I followed them niggas out to Lenox Mall, and they looked like they were getting ready to go to war."

"Word? So those niggas coming?"

"Naw, I saw your girl Nikki come outta the mall and start to talk to Dre's ass," Horse says.

"Really?"

"Yeah, son. Then she got in the car with him, and they broke out and drove to the Days Inn."

"You saw this shit?"

"Yeah, son, and your girl was all on his dick."

"A'ight . . . so she wanna get down like that? Cool, I'll hit you back in a minute Horse. One."

"One."

I hang up my phone.

It's not the money I spent on her ass—that was chump change. Even her fucking some other random dude is annoying, but understandable; she's a ho that strips. It's the principle of it all. Nikki thinking she can play me like that and go around fucking with the one nigga I got beef with is blatantly disrespectful, forcing a nigga to deal with that bitch accordingly.

"Fuck that ho," I say as I drive to Yvonne's house. I'm busy thinking of what I'm going to do to Nikki's ass when I catch up with her. Would Mo'Nique have disrespected me like that if she were my bitch? Naw, fuck that, she's just like her cousin. I'm gonna fuck her pretty ass as soon as I see her.

As I'm driving to the spot, I see Yvonne in the alley with some nigga. I slow up, park down the street, and creep back to the alley. Yvonne's begging for some dope from a young nigga that Corey got hustling for him. This bitch still hasn't paid me back for the shit she and her man Curtis stole from me.

"Please, just give me a little bit. I promise I'll pay you tomorrow," Yvonne says.

"Bitch, get the fuck away from me!" the kid snaps back.

"Come on, please?" she begs.

"Get the fuck outta here." This kid got potential, but then he gets soft on me.

"Please . . . I'll suck your dick," Yvonne pleads.

The kid stops and looks at her. "A'ight, that's what's up," he says. I gotta admit that when I was his age, I also used to let bitches suck me off for a hit. He unzips his pants and pulls out his dick. Yvonne inhales it in her mouth. Yvonne is sucking him off real good, too. After 10 minutes, the kid pulls out and zips up.

"Here." He throws her a nickel bag and walks away.

Yvonne snatches it up and sits right there, taking from her bag a spoon, a lighter, a candle, and a bottle of water. She holds the spoon over the f lame until the heroin melts, and then she dips the needle into the brown pool, slowly drawing the liquid until it fills the syringe. She taps it and then takes a belt out of her bag, wrapping it tight around her bicep. She finds the vein in her left arm that isn't completely dried up. She then carefully injects the dope in her arm and lets the rush get her high. She sits on the ground and leans against the wall, letting a wave of bliss take her over.

She's a dope fiend to the core. Damn shame. I hear this bitch used to have a good job at a law firm in midtown. Had a nice little frame on her, too: round ass and big tits. Now she looks like a scarecrow. I'm never gonna get my money back from this bitch. She's no better than Nikki's ass. I'm gonna have to put her outta her misery.

I head back to my car, pop the hood, and scrape some battery acid off, mixing it with some coke. Then I take a lighter out and cook it up in a cut-open soda can. I grab a hypodermic needle out of my glove compartment, draw up fifty CCs, and walk back to the alley.

Yvonne's still on cloud nine, high as a bitch. I walk up to her, and she looks up at me.

"Damien . . . I got . . . some money for you . . ."

"Don't worry about that, ma. You don't have to worry about that no more."

"I was gonna pay you back, Damien. It was Curtis's idea to do it," Yvonne says.

"I know. That's why I got something for you, because I know how loyal you are to me." I bend down and give her the needle.

"It's on me."

"Damien, you're too good to me. I swear I'm gonna get your money for you."

"I know, ma."

Yvonne finds the same vein and takes the lethal hit. At first she smiles, but the smile quickly turns into a look of fear as the dope begins to burn in her veins. Yvonne trembles profusely and foams from the mouth.

I stare in her eyes and smile as the bitch goes into convulsions and falls over on the ground. Pretty soon, she stops fidgeting and lies still. I can't help but think she got off easy compared to what I'm going to do to Nikki.

11

Worse Than Death

NIKKI

I end up staying the night with Dre in the hotel room. I enjoy being with him. I haven't enjoyed just kickin' it with a man in years. We stay up talking for the rest of the night about everything. I didn't realize Dre and I like a lot of the same things. It's weird . . . I almost forget that Dre's a trick. I think we're now on a different level than we were before.

I go to The Pink Palace that night, and it's thick as usual with the regular niggas that be in there. Penny's on stage doing her thing.

I've known Penny since the first day I started dancing. It's not often you find another girl in this game that you can trust. We look out for each other at all times. That's why we moved in together. Other than Mo'Nique, she's the only girl I fuck with up in here. When she got pregnant, her baby daddy wanted nothing to do with her, so Mo and I took care of her like family. All of the other girls know how we get down. Any of them start shit with any one of us, they get the beat down.

Penny's dancing to "Wait (the Whisper Song)." I come out on stage and start dancing with her. We're like the dynamic duo of stripping. We have a routine that makes it look like we're having sex on stage. These tricks give up mad dough to see us do it. While we're going through the motions, I start to feel sick. For some reason, my stomach's turning and I feel dizzy. Penny immediately senses that something's wrong with me.

"Nikki, what's wrong, girl?" Penny whispers to me.

"I don't know. . . . I'm just hot," I say as I continue to dance. The next thing I know, I'm flat on my ass.

"Nikki!" I hear Penny scream. One of the bouncers, Jon, picks me up and carries me backstage.

"Nikki, are you all right? Somebody call nine-one-one!" Penny yells as she strokes my face.

"I'm all right, Penny. What happened?"

"You fell the fuck out. How do you feel?"

"My stomach is upset."

"What did you eat?"

"I just ate some fried chicken before I got here."

"You probably got a little food poisoning," Penny says.

"I'm fine, I just—" I feel a surge come up my throat, and I vomit on the floor.

"Oh, shit! Oh, we gotta take you to the emergency room," Penny says. The way I'm feeling, I'm not gonna argue with her.

We go to Grady Memorial Hospital near the club. I'm in the ER lying on a bed. They draw some blood and run some tests on me. I feel better, but I want to know what happened to me. The doctor comes over to me.

"Well, Nicole, it appears that you don't have food poisoning," the doctor says.

"What? But I felt sick to my stomach."

"We got the results from your blood test back. You're pregnant."

It's like the world comes to a stop. I can't be pregnant, not by Damien or Dre. "I'm pregnant?"

"Yeah, I can give you some information. . . ." The doctor's words go in one ear and out the other. Penny and I bounce up outta there and back to the house.

"So, what are you gonna do?" Penny asks me.

"I ain't keeping it. I can't have a baby. Not from Dre, and especially not from Damien."

"Are you sure you wanna do that?"

"Penny, this ain't like Mike, the nigga that knocked you up. At least he pays child support. Dre's too immature and can't take care of a baby, and I wouldn't want any child with Damien as the father. I'm calling that abortion clinic in the morning and making an appointment."

"A'ight, girl, you know I got ya back. Are you gonna tell Mo?"

"Yeah, I'll give her a call."

I try to call Mo'Nique, but keep on getting her voicemail. It doesn't matter anyway. I'm not going to have this fucking baby. That's the last thing I need to have now. Dre is still a little boy running the streets. Although he would love for me to have his baby, I can't depend on him. Hell, he's planning on going to war with Damien and getting his ass killed. Damien's a trick to the third power. He already got a baby up north. I don't wanna have any ties to him like that. If I plan on getting with King, I can't have Damien's baby. I can't believe I let myself get so careless and let one of them mutherfuckas knock me up! Besides, I ain't letting no baby mess up my body and give me stretch marks and shit.

The next day, I go to the clinic and meet with a doctor who explains the procedure of the operation to me. Turns out I'm just two weeks pregnant, so it must be Damien's. She's talking to me as if this would be one of the hardest decisions in my life and that I might have some regrets. Shit, there ain't nothing more I want than to get this damn baby outta me. I tell her that I don't care how they do it, I just want to get this over and done with. I set a date for next week to have it done.

I'm heading back home when I get a call from Damien. Great, this is the last nigga I want to talk to. I have to play it cool. I don't want him to think that anything's wrong. I answer my phone and talk to him.

"Hey, baby, what's up?"

"Nothing, ma. I just wanted to know what you were doing," Damien says.

"Nothing right now. I'm just heading back to my house."

"Good. I was about to head over to your house."

Oh, that's just great.

"Good, I been missing you. I'll see you there in a minute," I lie.

"A'ight, ma." Damien hangs up.

I'm not really in the mood to see Damien, especially after the morning I just had, but I have to suck it up and hustle this trick. When I get to my house, Damien is already there, waiting for me. Damn, he must really want some ass to be here already. I should tell him about Dre getting ready to come after him, but knowing Damien, he would go after him first. The more I think about it, if Dre did kill Damien, then that would free me up to go after King. I really like Dre, but King got that serious paper. I'll just wait and see how things play themselves out.

"Hey, baby," I say to Damien as I kiss him.

"Hey, ma. So you been missing me?" he asks.

"Of course. Who else is going to do me like you?"

"Nobody. Come on, I wanna take you somewhere."

"A'ight, where we going?" I ask him.

"Just a little spot I got in the cut up in College Park," Damien says.

"A'ight."

I get in his truck, and we drive to College Park. As we drive to the house, I wonder to myself what Damien would do if I told him I was pregnant. Would he be happy, or cuss me out and deny it? He says he's never fucked with a girl that looks like me before, but would he want me to have his baby? Oh, well, I guess we'll never know. After I have this abortion, I gotta figure out a way to get King alone and put it on him.

We exit off the highway and on to Riverdale Road and drive down to Flat Shoals Road to a little house down the street.

"This is where you wanted to take me, Damien?" I ask him as I get out of the car.

"Yeah, ma."

"Why? It looks like a traphouse. Why can't we just go to your place?"

"Naw, I got niggas over there handling business."

We go inside the house, and it's not as shitty as it looked from the outside. It kinda looks like somebody's house with all the pictures on the wall. Oh, well. I don't care. We can do it anywhere.

We walk into a bedroom, and Damien closes the door behind him. Damien unzips his pants and pulls out his dick.

"Come here, ma."

Damien loves the way I give him head. I gave him head so good once that he bought me a $3,000 tennis bracelet from Tiffany's. Let's see if I can get him to buy me a car today. I'm sucking his dick like a milkshake, taking in as much of his dick as I can, slurping on his meat.

"Oh, shit . . . yeah. Suck this dick . . . Ah . . ." Damien mumbles as he places his hand behind my head. He's really getting into it now. Damien starts to move his hips back and forth and places both hands behind my head.

"Yeah, bitch, suck this dick." Damn, he's shoving his dick down my throat so hard that it feels like I'm about to suffocate!

A'ight, enough of this. I know it's good, but this nigga is about to choke the shit outta me. I pull my head back and take him out of my mouth.

"Damn, Damien, you trying to kill me?"

"Naw, ma . . . it just felt so good."

"A'ight, just take it easy."

I pull off my clothes and lie naked on the queen-sized bed. Damien gets on top of me and spreads my legs like a wishbone. He rams his dick into my pussy and starts to hump away. He's being really aggressive today. He's fucking me like he ain't never had no pussy before.

"Slow down, baby," I say to him, but he ignores me as he bites on my nipples.

"Ow! Damien, what the fuck!"

Damien ignores me again and keeps on going. After about an hour in the missionary position, I start to get tired of Damien pounding my pussy like a madman.

"Damien, I'm tired."

Damien then pulls out and flips me over and rams his dick back in me doggie style. "Come here, bitch," Damien says as he digs into me with his powerful, hard thrusts.

Okay, I know some niggas get caught up in the moment, but that's enough with the "bitch" comments.

"Damien, stop . . . Come on . . . stop."

"Shut up, bitch."

"What? Oh, hell naw! Get the fuck off of me." I try to get up, but Damien puts his body weight on me, and I collapse under his bulk

"You love dick, don't ya? You like to fuck, huh? Well, we gonna fuck! Just like you fucked Dre's punk ass!"

Oh, shit! He knows about Dre and me. Oh God, is he gonna kill me?

"Damien please, it's not what you think," I say to him, but Damien ignores me and punishes me even more with his short, hard dick strokes. I think I start to bleed because I'm so dry, but Damien doesn't stop.

I'm gonna die. This crazy nigga is going to kill me. That's all I can think as the pain becomes unbearable. Damien finally pulls out of me and stands up. My pussy is so sore. Damien grabs my shirt and wipes the blood off his dick and throws it in my face.

"Damien . . ."

"Shut the fuck up." Damien backhands me, and I fall back against the bed.

"You thought you could play me and fuck the one nigga I got beef with down here."

My face is still stinging from his blow. "Damien, listen to me—"

"You ain't nothing but a ho anyway."

"Damien, listen. I'm pregnant."

Damien looks at me then laughs. "Bitch, who you think you playing? I don't give a fuck."

Oh God, he's got no reason to believe me.

"Are you gonna kill me?"

"Kill you? Naw, I ain't gonna kill you. You see, I've gotten kinda poetic with this revenge shit now. So since you like to fuck so much, that's exactly what you gonna do."

Damien opens the door, and Horse walks in.

"Oh, hell no. I ain't doing shit with him." I try to get up, and *CRACK!* Damien punches me in the side of my head and knocks the shit outta me. I bounce off the bed and hit the floor. Then he stomps me in my stomach. I scream in pain and see Damien towering above me like a demon. All I can think about is my baby. I'm gonna lose my baby.

"What did you tell me? You know some bitches that would fuck Horse like Tyson Beckford? Well, guess what? You that bitch," Damien says with a smile on his face. "Have fun, my nigga."

"A'ight, son," Horse says as Damien leaves.

Horse unbuckles his belt and pulls down his pants, grabbing his dick. Oh shit, I see why they call this nigga Horse.

"Get up," Horse demands.

Damien has knocked what little fight I have outta me. My pussy's really sore, and I think it's torn. My face is throbbing with pain, and I'm barely conscious after Damien's punch. I curl up in the fetal position, scared to death.

"Get up, bitch!" Horse yells. I don't move. Horse reaches down and grabs me by my hair, pulling me up and throwing me on the bed.

"Oww!" This foul nigga weighs at least 350 pounds, and he's flopping on top of me like it's nothing.

"I've wanted your ass for so long now." Horse forces my legs open, hurting my inner thighs. Then he shoves his dick into my battered pussy.

Horse begins humping me like a wild dog in heat. All I can do is lay there silently and cry as Horse's big, fat, smelly ass violates me repeatedly. The pain is excruciating as I feel blood flow down my legs. Horse kisses my neck, then sucks and bites my nipples. I'm in pure torture while Horse is having the time of his life.

Horse pulls out of me and flips me over. I think that he wants to do me doggie style, but instead he rams his huge dick in my ass. I scream and try to pull away.

"Aaarrrggghhh! Take it out!" Then I feel a painful blow to the back of my head.

I must have blacked out for a few minutes. I awake to pain and the rank stench of shit and blood in the air. I'm lying flat on my stomach and can hear Horse's fat ass huffing and puffing as he continues to pound my rectum. He must've hurt me internally, because I lose control of my bowels, and my ass explodes liquid shit all over Horse's dick and stomach.

"Hey! You nasty-ass bitch!" Horse pulls up off me and punches me in the ribs, knocking the wind outta me. "Stinking bitch!" Horse hits me again across the face.

The last thing I remember is him pissing on me and then I black out again. I almost wish that Damien had killed me.

12

The Block is Hot

JAYSON

I drive to Decatur at about 9:30 p.m. to meet up with Lt. McNiven. I fill him in on the meeting going down this Saturday night. It's time to end this so I can go back to just being Jayson Harper again, so I can be with Janelle for real. Look at me. I'm a cop in love with an ex-stripper. How funny is that?

"King says the deal is going to go down Saturday night, but he's keeping the details of where and when to himself until the last moment," I tell him.

"Are you sure about this? We'll have to watch you from a distance then."

"Yeah, it's going down. He's been talking to his contact, Simon, out in L.A. for months now. King's paying them ten million for the coke."

"Ten million? This is the biggest deal I've ever seen. Once it hits the streets, it's gonna triple in value."

"Exactly. This is what we've been waiting for—taking these mutherfuckas down. I can also get Damien on at least two murders and a rape charge."

"Rape charge on whom?" he asks.

"Janelle. He tried to rape her."

"Really, and what did you do?"

"Nothing, I just got her out of town."

"Where?"

"Savannah."

McNiven looks at me oddly, and I know what he's thinking.

"Why would you send her to Savannah, of all places? Does she know who you are?"

"Yeah, she does."

"Oh my God, you blow your cover to a girl connected to the fucking people we're about to bust?"

"She's not connected to them!"

"You don't know that for sure! My God, Jayson. You've not only put this operation, but also your damn life on the line over this girl! I'm pulling you out."

"What? Lieutenant, you can't do that!"

"The hell I can't! You've compromised yourself."

"No, I haven't! Listen, you've never had anyone as deep as me. If you pull me out now, King will cancel the deal and you'll never be able to bring him down like this! You cannot throw six months of police work out the window for something that I got under control, and you know it!"

McNiven turns around and looks at me. He knows that I'm right. "Okay, we'll go ahead, but after this case is completed, you're done with undercover work."

"I know. I'm quitting the force after this."

"What? Why?" he asks.

"Lieutenant, I've given ten years of my life to this job. It has cost me my marriage and pretty much my life without anything to show for it. I got a chance now to be with a woman that I love. I'm not gonna lose her, too."

"You're serious about this?"

"Dead serious."

"All right, if that's your decision. Saturday morning you'll get a wire and we'll get this done," he says.

"Good." I turn and walk to my car and drive off. As soon as this is done, I'm gonna start being Jayson Harper again.

When I get to my place, I see Quan parked in front of my townhouse. I pull up next to him and get out.

"What's up, Quan?"

"Yo, man, I think you need to come with me," Quan says gravely.

"What's going on?"

"Yo, Damien and them are doing some real foul shit, man."

"What are you talking about, man?"

"Ya girl, Nikki . . . Damien found out about her messing around with Dre behind his back."

"Oh, shit. What did he do?"

"Yo, he brought Corey and me over there and told us to do whatever we wanted with her, and then he bounced. We were wondering what the hell he was talking about, until we went inside and saw your girl tied to the bed, fucked up on some medieval shit. Corey went in, but I broke the fuck outta there, man."

"Where is she now?"

"She's at Yvonne's house over on Flat Shoals."

We drive over there and go into the house and walk to the bedroom. When we walk in, the stench of waste knocks us over.

"Oh God," I utter. I see Nikki unconscious, naked, and tied to the bed. She's bloodied and bruised, lying in her own feces.

"Yo, should I call the paramedics?" Quan asks.

"No, we need to go now. Give me a wet towel from the bathroom."

Quan gets the towel, and I clean her off. Damn, Damien's a sick fucker for doing this to her. Oh my God, she looks like she was gang-raped and beaten to a pulp. There is a lot of blood between her legs, but she still has a pulse.

I rush her in my car to Southern Regional Hospital on Upper Riverdale Road. The doctors rush her to the emergency room and put her in the intensive care unit. They say she has severe internal hemorrhaging and is still unconscious. She is in critical condition. The doctor says that she was pregnant and suffered a miscarriage as a result of the trauma her body went through. They need to operate in order to remove the fetus.

Here comes the worst part: I have to tell Janelle what happened to her cousin.

DAMIEN

This is the way it should be done. Real niggas handle they business quickly and thoroughly. It's time for me to step on all these little roaches and rats running around me. First Yvonne's crack head, then Nikki's slut ass, and now

Dre's bitch ass. No need to tell King about this shit; this is strictly off the books. I woulda told Tommy, but he woulda only tried to talk me outta doing this now. Tommy's my nigga, but I can't let these bitches down here front on me.

I take Corey, Horse and 10 other niggas we got working for us to the Bankhead projects that Dre is hustling out of. I take out my trusty AK-47 and make sure I have four extra clips ready to go. We roll up to the spot Dre's black Cadillac DeVille is parked in front of and wait to see him. Corey approaches from the other end to box these niggas in.

It's nightfall, and the corner boys are working the spot while another nigga stands across the street and keeps a lookout for five-o. I make sure all three cars we drive don't stick out so we can creep this nigga.

Dre is still supervising the operation, which is small compared to mine. I just wanna make sure I blast this nigga this time.

What's this dumb nigga doing? Corey's car starts to move up on the corner with his lights off. Shit! Not yet, ma'fucker!

One of the corner boys spots Corey's car creeping up and pulls out his gun and starts to blast his car. Corey sticks his nine out of the window and starts to spit shells, hitting two of them.

Damn, I didn't even see Dre's ass yet and this fool starts blasting!

I drive up from the other end of the street and let the AK spit at these niggas. I hit the lookout boy and open his chest up. Then that ma'fucker Dre comes out of the alley in back of the house with a submachine gun and starts to spray up Corey's car. I'm not sure, but I think Corey gets hit. The driver's side is Swiss-cheesed up real good.

My nigga Horse starts to bust his .44 Magnum at Dre and hits a nigga next to him. The other nigga in Corey's car takes over and pulls off. I bust my AK at Dre, but this nigga gets cover behind the house. Shit! This is not how this shit was supposed to go down.

I mash down on the gas and get the hell outta there before the police show up. I bend the corner and run a red light and get on the highway. How many lives does that ma'fucker Dre have? I swear, I'm gonna kill Corey's punk ass for fucking this up.

We pull off the highway and go under an overpass. I jump out and walk over to Corey's car.

"What the fuck did you think you were doing, nigga?" I say as I open the driver's door. I see another nigga driving and Corey dead on the passenger's side.

"Fuck! Get outta the car and get in the truck!" I yell at the nigga in the car.

"What about Corey?" Horse asks.

"What about him? That nigga's dead. Let's go!"

We leave Corey and his car under the overpass and get back on the highway. We head back to College Park. Shit! This whole hit went up in smoke just like that. At least we got four of them niggas. King is gonna flip when this shit gets back to him. Oh, well. He's just another roach I gotta step on.

When I get back to my spot, Tommy is there waiting for me. "What the hell is going on, Dame?" Tommy says. Tommy is the only cat I know that's never backed down to me. Either I'm gonna have him by my side running this shit, or I'm gonna have to kill him one day.

"What you think? I had to get at Dre before he got at us."

"What about Nikki? What the fuck was that about?" Tommy asks me.

"That's what happens to people who cross me, Tommy. Remember that. Listen, Tommy, you my man and I got love for you, my nigga, but things are going to change, and you gonna have to pick a side. Either you ride with me, or I ride over you. What's it gonna be?" I say to Tommy as I stare at him in the eyes.

"I told you once, Dame, we ride together, we die together. I'm a man of my word," Tommy says.

"That's all I needed to hear, my nigga."

13

Too Good to Last

JANELLE

I've been at Jayson's apartment in Savannah for two days. It's not that different from his townhouse in College Park, except for the pictures of his family and this woman in most of these pictures with him. I'm gonna assume that this is Lauren, his ex-wife. It's so weird seeing Jayson in these pictures. He seems so different. It's like he's a totally different person than who I know in Atlanta.

After looking at the photos of Lauren and seeing the kind of woman Vanessa is, I wonder what it is he sees in me. I'm nothing like Vanessa. I don't wanna be anything like her, but it makes me wonder why Jayson wants me. Am I just a rebound thing he's using to get over his ex-wife? Or does he just feel sorry for me?

Stop it, Janelle. He loves me. I don't need to question it; I know it. The way he holds me. The way he kisses me. Hell, he told me he was a cop. He didn't have to do that. For all he knew, I coulda turned around and told Damien.

I've been so worried about him since I found out, like I know something is going to go wrong and I'm going to lose him. Damien is crazy. He doesn't care what he does. I know that King is the big boss, but Damien scares me more than he does. I just want Jayson and me to be together. I don't care what happens to Damien or King. I just want him in my arms.

We can just go to Florida and start our lives over together. Jayson doesn't have to be an undercover cop, and I don't have to be the ex-stripper everybody stares at. I can just be me. I can be Janelle for a change. I wish it were all that simple.

Since I had to come here, I pretty much gave up my job at Harland. I can still take my classes online and complete my GED. I've been thinking that I want to go to college—to do what there, I have no idea. These past few days I've been thinking a lot more about what I wanna do. I still can't make up my mind. I've been watching MTV and BET most of the day here anyway. Real productive, I know.

My cell phone starts to ring, and I see Tommy's name pop up.

"Hello, Jayson?"

"Hey . . ." I can tell something's wrong by the sound of his voice.

"What's wrong, Jayson?" I ask him.

"You gotta come back to Atlanta, baby," Jayson says to me, and I know it can't be good.

"Why, what happened?"

"Nikki . . . she's been hurt."

"Oh God, what happened to her?"

"Just drive back to Atlanta."

"What happened to her?"

"She's been hurt pretty bad by Damien," Jayson says.

The next few minutes are a blur. I somehow manage to get in my car and start to drive back to Atlanta. How could I have been so stupid to leave Nikki with that psycho Damien? I should have told her what he did to me. I should have warned her. I was just thinking of myself when I shoulda been helping her. I knew her being with Damien was dangerous. Shit!

My mind is blown as I start to head toward Southern Regional Hospital. When I get there, I see Jayson and Quan in the lobby waiting for me. Jayson walks toward me and I hug him.

"What happened to her, Tommy?"

"Before you go in there . . . it's not good. She was raped and beaten."

"Damien . . ."

"Yeah." We walk to her room, and I'm scared to see her. We get to the door, and Jayson lets me go in alone. Oh my God, Nikki is swollen up so much that I don't even recognize her. Her cheeks are so puffy, and all kinds of tubes are running into her. She's still unconscious.

I take her hand and start to cry. My God, how could he do this to her? I knew she was playing a dangerous game with him. I'm gonna kill him. I swear by everything I hold dear, I'm going to kill that sick son of a bitch for doing this to her. This is worse than what happened to me as a kid. Jayson told me Horse also raped her. That fat fucker is gonna wish he never even looked in her direction.

"Nikki, you're going to be okay, girl. I'm so sorry . . . I should have been here for you. You just need to rest and get better. You hear me? I promise you that I'm going to make sure Damien and Horse pay for this."

The tears just flow down my face, and I can't help but think that this could have easily been me. Damien's a sick dog for doing this, and he's got to be put down. I don't care what I have to do to get him.

I walk outta her room and see Jayson waiting for me. He hugs me, and I break down in his arms and cry.

"I'm sorry this happened," Jayson says.

"Don't be. Just make sure you get his ass for this."

"I will."

Quan is standing to the side.

"I'm going to go see what's going on. You're gonna stay here?" Jayson asks.

"Yeah."

"Quan, can you stay here with her and make sure she's all right?"

"Sure, no problem," Quan replies. For some reason, Quan is different from the others, and I trust him.

"Be careful," I say to Jayson.

"I will, baby. She'll be fine."

"I hope so." I give Jayson a kiss before he goes.

JAYSON

I leave Janelle at the hospital with Quan. There's no way she's going to leave Nikki's side tonight. I get a call from Lt. McNiven. They found Corey's body in a car on the side of the highway on 285. He also told me that five of Dre's homeboys were taken to the morgue this morning. The shit had hit the fan. Dre's going to come at Damien with everything he's got. This is the kind of shit we don't need to have happen before the deal. Obviously King is thinking the same thing when he calls me.

"What the fuck happened, Tommy?" King says to me over the phone.

"Damien tried to hit Dre and shit went ugly."

"What the fuck was he thinking? I've been blowing up this nigga's cell for the past three hours and he hasn't called me back!" King yells.

"I don't know. He didn't tell me he was going to do this."

"I told him no fuckups and he goes and pulls this!"

"I'll try and catch up with him," I tell him.

"No, come over here. We gotta figure out how much damage this nigga's done," King says.

"All right. I'll be there."

I drive to King's spot in Buckhead, and I get the feeling shit is gonna get a lot worse before it gets better. The one thing that keeps on playing in my head is what Damien said to me: *Things are going to change, and you gonna have to pick a side.* What's that nigga up to? This nigga Damien is ill enough to do anything—would he turn on King? I gotta get Vanessa outta there before shit gets really fucked up.

I get to King's place and go inside. I see him pacing back and forth, smoking a blunt.

"Tommy, we need to talk."

"Okay."

He gives me some dap. "What's wrong with this nigga?"

"I don't know. He found out his girl Nikki was messing with Dre, and he flipped out and ran a gang-rape on her."

"You mean he flipped out like this over some bitch? You know, I thought Damien was smart enough to handle shit on his own. That's why I let him run shit down here," King says to me as he takes another puff of his blunt.

"I don't think you made a mistake. I just think this Dre cat got under his skin," I tell him.

"You a good dude, Tommy, but Dame ain't ready for what's about to go down. This nigga ain't thinking straight. You wouldn't let no bitch make you fuck up like this," King says.

If only you knew, nigga.

"Naw, I wouldn't."

"Look, Tommy, this deal that's about to go down is gonna put us on a whole new level. I can't have Dame doing shit like this."

"What are you saying?"

"What I'm saying, Tommy, is that I've been checking you out for the past few months and you're the type of nigga I need by my side to help me run this shit," King says.

"What about Dame?" I ask.

"Dame is my nigga, and I'll always have love for him, but this is business. Everybody gotta play they part." King's phone rings.

"Yo, pour yourself up a drink, my nigga. I gotta take this outside."

"A'ight."

Ain't this some shit? He trusts me. King is ready to replace Damien with me. It would be a smart move, too, if I wasn't cop. This is exactly the position I've been trying to put myself in for the past six months. So why do I still got this rotten feeling in my gut? If Damien meant what he said to me, then things are not going to go as smoothly as King thinks.

I take a drink of brandy and Vanessa walks in the room, looking more stunning than I remembered.

"Jayson, something's wrong, isn't it?" Vanessa asks me.

"Why do you say that?"

"King, he's been pissed off about what Damien did last night."

"Yeah, Damien's out of control. He raped and beat Nikki to a pulp."

"Oh my God, is she all right?"

"She still hasn't regained consciousness."

"I can't wait for this to be over. I can't wait for us to be together," Vanessa says as she caresses my arm.

"Vanessa, I'm going to protect you and make sure you're okay, but after this is over, we can't be together."

"Why not?"

"There's somebody else in my life now."

"Mo'Nique? The little stripper girl? You can't be for real, Jayson."

"There's more to her than that. I care about you, Vanessa, but I'm not in love with you."

"And you're in love with her? This is ridiculous, Jayson. We have a past together that's much deeper than what she has with *Tommy*," Vanessa says sarcastically.

"It's in the past, and what I got with her is real."

Vanessa pulls away from me. "The other night when we made love, was that the past too?" she asks.

"No, that was our night, but it's not what—it was just one night. I'm sorry if I led you on, Vanessa, but I really do care about Janelle."

"Oh, it's Janelle now? If she's what you want, Jayson, then I'm not going to get in your way." Vanessa turns around and walks out of the door.

Great, another woman that hates my guts. I didn't want to hurt her. She's the last person I wanted to hurt, but I can't let her think that we have a future together. This is just another reason why I'm going to quit this job.

14

A Woman Scorned

DAMIEN

King has been blowing up my phone all day, so I guess it's time I see him face to face. My contact told me that Tommy's at his house in Buckhead, so all the major players are in place. I know what King is thinking. I know him better than anyone else does. I know him better than he thinks, as a matter of fact. He thinks that I'm bugging out because of Nikki and Dre, when in fact that was just me having fun. He's probably telling Tommy how unstable I am and that he wants him to take my place. "Everybody has to play their part." He loves to say that shit.

He always used to say that to me, even when we were kids. King has always underestimated me, treating me like a frontline solider on the corner instead of the partner who helped him muscle out the competition. I admit that King was always street smart, and that he did start shit up. He was a hustler, for sure—"Was" being the key word—before he got all soft and shit. It's time to change the game.

Like I said before, I'm a loyal nigga, but if you fuck me, I'm gonna fuck you right back. King has always been shady when it comes to money and other things he's kept from me. I never used to say anything about it because he was the brains behind the hustle and you don't bite the hand that feeds you, but you would think that after all this time my nigga would do me right. I guess I just gotta take what's mine.

I pull up to the house and see Tommy's Cadillac out front. I walk up and a maid lets me in. I see King outside on the terrace on the phone. He turns around and sees me.

"Dame, what the hell is going on with you?" he says as he hangs up.

"Nothing, just tying up some loose ends," I say.

"Some loose ends? You go and shoot up a project in Bankhead and kill five niggas and that's tying up some loose ends? What the fuck are you thinking?" King yells.

"You know, my nigga, you don't sound like a hustler anymore. You starting to sound a little soft to me."

"Soft? Nigga, have you lost your mutherfuckin' mind? I've run this shit from the start!"

"And I erased everybody that got in our way. From day one, I've been your man, and yet you still treat me like some cornball nigga standing on the block. You still think I'm some stupid-ass nigga you can feed breadcrumbs to and have me do all the dirty work," I tell him.

"So, this is what this is all about? You feel underappreciated?" King says.

"As a matter of fact, I do. I feel about ten million dollars underappreciated, my nigga."

"You want more money? Nigga, we about to make millions!"

"No, you about to make millions, while you continue to pay me like a corner boy. Ever since I was a kid you've always treated me like I was under you. Never like your partner. Well, I think it's time things changed." I pull out my .45 and point it at him.

"What's this? You taking over? You gonna kill me? You think you can do what I do?"

"I've been in this game a long time. I know more than you think, including your bank account numbers and about Bishop."

King looks at me surprised, but then realizes where I got my info. "I should have known. So this is how you gonna do it? We've been down for over fifteen years, Dame, and this is how you do me? I thought we were dawgs, my nigga."

"We are. This is just business."

I put a slug in King's chest and he drops dead.

Tommy comes rushing outside with his gun in his hand. "What the fuck is going on?" Tommy says, stunned.

"I told you, Tommy, either you're with me or against me. So are you with me?" I ask him with my gun still in my hand.

"Yeah, I just wish you would've told me what you had in mind."

"Sometimes you gotta make moves in silence, my nigga."

"What about the deal with the L.A. connection?" Tommy asks.

"That's still gonna go down. Just think of this as a little corporate restructuring," I tell him.

"Shit, Wall Street ain't never seen no shit like this, but I don't think the L.A. connection is gonna like the sudden change."

"That's already been taken care of."

"What do you mean? King's been dealing with them for months now," Tommy says.

"Who do you think helped King get in contact with those West Coast suppliers?" I say.

"Who?"

"Me," Vanessa says as she points a gun at Tommy's head.

"Vanessa, what are you doing?" Tommy asks, surprised.

"You always were too trusting, Jayson. Drop the gun," Vanessa says.

"Yo, chill with all that. Tommy's down with me," I tell her.

"Tommy's a cop," Vanessa reveals.

"What the fuck are you talking about?"

"His real name is Officer Jayson Harper. He's been undercover in Atlanta for six months now, getting close to you," Vanessa says as Tommy looks at her, stunned.

"What the fuck? A cop? Why didn't you tell me that shit before?" I yell at her, pointing my gun at him.

"Because I have a history with him," Vanessa says.

"You've been working with Damien this whole time. You've been playing me since the beginning," Tommy growls at Vanessa.

"That's right. Damien and I have been planning this deal for months now, waiting for King to give us access to his offshore accounts. I didn't expect to see you with Damien. I was going to cut you in, Jayson, but you chose that bitch Mo'Nique over me."

"Vanessa, this is crazy. You don't think you're going to get away with this?"

"Of course we will, Jayson. You're not even wired, and it appears that King figured out who you were, and you were forced to defend yourself and shoot him. Unfortunately, King was able to get a shot off and he killed you, too," Vanessa explains.

"You're a fucking cop? Damn, you had me fooled, my nigga."

"I can't believe I thought you loved me, Vanessa," Tommy says.

"I do, Jayson, but you know what they say about a woman scorned."

Thunder explodes from the end of Vanessa's gun. Tommy falls to the ground.

Ain't that a bitch. And I thought I was cold blooded.

JANELLE

Seeing Nikki like this really puts things in perspective for me. The life that we're living, the things we're doing just to get a dollar from a nigga ain't worth this. The doctors let me stay the night in her room. I call Penny and tell her what happened, and she tells me that she will be there first thing in the morning. I hope Jayson is able to end this shit soon. I fall asleep in the chair next to her bed.

"Hey. Wake up," Nikki whispers to me.

"Nikki! Oh, girl, you had me so damn scared."

"I'm . . . sorry, M," Nikki says softly as tears roll down her face.

"You don't have anything to be sorry for," I tell her as I wipe her tears away.

"I do. You were right . . . about the life I was living. You did the . . . the right thing by getting out."

"It's okay now, Nikki. I'm gonna take care of you."

"I was wrong to be angry with you," Nikki says.

"It's okay, Nikki."

Nikki goes back to sleep a few minutes later. At least she woke up. The doctors told me that her body would heal, but I'm more concerned about her mind. They told me she was pregnant. I know Nikki wasn't going to keep it, but I also know that she didn't want to lose it like this. Shit couldn't get any worse—or at least that's what I thought.

Quan comes into Nikki's room at about three o'clock in the morning and wakes me up.

"Mo'Nique, wake up," Quan says softly.

"What is it?"

"I just called Tommy's cell and a police officer answered it."

"What did they say?" I ask, already knowing it can't be good.

"At first they wouldn't tell me what was going on, but then I said I was Tommy's brother, and they told me he's been taken to St. Joseph's Hospital."

"Oh, shit!" My heart's racing. I know something awful has happened to Jayson.

I leave Southern Regional Hospital with Quan and rush to the north side of Atlanta to another damn hospital. When we get there, I rush into the emergency room entrance and speak to the unit secretary.

"Excuse me. Do you have a Tommy Holloway here?"

The desk secretary looks at me funny. "Ma'am, I'm not allowed to give out any information on any patient brought into the ER," she says.

"We were told Tommy was brought here an hour ago!" I yell at her.

"I'm sorry, ma'am, but if you have a seat, I can find somebody you can talk to."

"Listen, his real name is Jayson Harper. He's an undercover cop," I tell her.

"What? Tommy's a cop?" Quan says in shock. Then a white man walks over to me.

"Are you Janelle Taylor?" he asks.

"Yeah, who are you?"

"I'm John McNiven, Jayson's commanding officer," he says.

"What happened to Jayson? Is he okay?"

McNiven looks at me then says it. "The police department got a call that they heard shots fired at a house in Buckhead. When the police and paramedics arrived, they found Jayson shot in the abdomen."

"No . . ." I say, not wanting to accept it.

"Listen, Jayson was rushed here and has been in surgery. The doctors said that his chances are pretty good. The paramedics got him here in time," McNiven tells me.

"Who did it?" I ask.

"It appears that Jayson shot and killed Dwayne Smith, but he was able to get a shot off."

"What about Damien?"

"We're still looking for him at this time. Janelle, I know Jayson told you who he was and that you care a lot for him. We're going to do everything we can to find out what happened to him," he says. He puts his hand on my shoulder and then walks away.

I already know in my heart that Damien is behind this. King didn't have any reason to shoot Jayson. Damien was the one running around out of control. And where the hell is Vanessa? She just disappears with Damien all of a sudden? I knew this would happen. I knew things wouldn't go down so easy, not with that asshole Damien on the loose like this. Now all I can do is pray that Jayson pulls through this. First Nikki, now him—I can't deal with all this.

Quan and I sit in the waiting room together, and I can tell he's still surprised. Hell, it freaked me out when Jayson told me. I know Quan might be thinking that he's gonna be arrested now, but I got a feeling Jayson likes him and won't let him go down.

"You know, out of everybody, you were the one person he didn't want to see get caught up in all this," I tell him.

"Yeah, he always used to tell me I was smarter than this. Now I know why. How long have you known?"

"He told me a couple of weeks ago."

"Wow, he must be really in love with you to do that."

"Yeah, I guess so. So, what do you think really happened, Quan?"

"I don't think King shot Jayson. If we didn't know Tommy, I mean Jayson, was a cop, he wouldn't either, and Damien for sure didn't know," he says.

"But I know somebody else that did know. Vanessa."

"Really . . . and now she's gone and so is Damien. Sounds like a conspiracy to me."

"Me too." I never did like that bitch, and I bet she had something to do with this or else she would be here now. She probably played on Jayson's old feelings for her and told him some sob story.

Another hour goes by before the doctors tell us that Jayson pulled through the surgery and is in stable condition. I guess one way or another things are over, but karma is a bitch, and sooner or later it's going to catch up with Damien and Vanessa.

15

Industry Gangsta

Harlem, New York

DAMIEN

New York, New York. It feels good to be home, baby, and it feels even better to be rich. Anybody that says money can't buy happiness is a broke-ass ma'fucker! Ain't nothing better than getting thirty-five million in my bank account.

Been back up in Harlem for a week, keeping a low profile. Sure, this plan I had with Vanessa was some scheming-ass shit, but it was worth it. I can't believe we hustled the biggest hustler in New York. But I can't laugh too hard, because the nigga I thought I could call my main man turned out to be a fuckin' cop! Tommy had my ass fooled good. That nigga should get an Academy Award for his performance.

Between the way Vanessa played King and the way Tommy, or should I say Officer Harper, fooled me, that shit just shows me that you can't trust anybody. Fuck that, I ain't messing with nobody brand new. Period. Horse is a good nigga to have in the street, but I need to rebuild my inner circle. I know just who I have in mind, too: my cousin Rob out in Brooklyn.

I ride to Flatbush and see my nigga working a dead block. Last I heard, Rob got outta the joint three months ago. I know how it is to get out and have no money and nobody ain't trying to give you a job. The only thing you can do is get a half-ounce rock and start slinging that shit.

"Yo, Rob!" I yell at him.

He looks and sees me standing next to the black S500 I picked up two days ago. "My nigga, Dame," Rob says as he walks over to me.

"What's up, cuz?" I say as I give him some dap.

"I'm just out here grindin', yo, doing my thing."

"So I see."

"Yo, when did you get back in New York?" he asks.

"Just a week ago. I've been down south making moves."

"Yeah, I heard your man King got hit, son," Rob says.

"You heard about that shit up here?"

"You know how shit flows in New York. Walls have ears," he says.

"I guess they do. Yo, my nigga, the block doesn't look too hot."

"Yeah, man, niggas ain't getting high like they used to. I'm kinda fucked up in the game right now. So you running the Flip Set?" he asks.

"Yeah, I'm the man. So let me ask you, son, you making money now?"

Rob's got pride, and no nigga wanna admit they ain't making money, but he ain't stupid enough to let an opportunity pass him by. "I've been doing better, yo."

"So do you really wanna make this money?"

"What you flippin', nigga?" Rob asks.

"I ain't talking about being a corner boy. Yo, you family, son, and I don't like to see my peoples out here fucked up. Listen, I need a good nigga by my side to help me run this empire," I tell him.

"Listen, Dame, I'm hungry and I'm trying to eat, so whatever you need, man, I got you," Rob says.

I look in his eye and I see that he's for real. "All right man, take this." I hit him off with three grand in his hand.

"Whoa."

"Get yourself cleaned up and get some new gear. Call me tomorrow and I'm gonna put you on to some major game."

"All right, yo, good looking," Rob says and counts the money I gave him.

"Yo, one." I get in my ride and bounce.

Rob's a good dude. He knows how to handle himself. I got Horse directing traffic on the corners in Harlem. I'm gonna put Rob under my wing and make him my lieutenant. I ain't gonna lose touch with the street like King did. King wanted to kick back too much and be a Don running shit, but that was his downfall. You gotta stay focused and watch these niggas that be close to you, making sure they be doing what they supposed to do, 'cause they might be thinking about smokin' you.

Like I told King, it's never personal. Nowadays it's the way. You know how niggas get knocked when they try and go beyond they comfort zone, like how King was trying to lock down the whole East Coast. The feds don't like that shit. That's when you get these *Miami Vice* niggas, like Tommy, trying to bring you down. I'm happy being a big fish in small lake.

It's time I go see my seed, Taye, and my BM, Trina. I've been missing my son. I gotta make sure he knows who his daddy is. Plus, I gotta let

Trina know daddy's home and tap that ass. I'm over that Nikki bitch. It's time to fuck with my number one. Ain't no chick like the one I got.

I drive back to Harlem's West 138th Street in Hamilton Heights to Trina's home and park in the back like usual. Trina looks out the window and sees me and opens the door.

"I heard you were back. It's about time you came through," Trina says.

"You miss me, baby?"

"Yeah, I missed you." Trina is wearing a tight little black spaghetti-strap dress. I walk up to her and kiss her lips and my dick gets hard. Damn, I didn't realize that I missed her so much.

"Where's Taye?"

"He's at my mommy's house," she says as she turns and walks inside the house. I follow her. She knows what she's doing by wearing that shit around me. She bends over to turn on the stereo and she isn't wearing any panties. Damn, that pussy is so fat.

"I got that money you sent me. Where did you get that much cash from?" Trina asks.

"It was just a little pocket change to take care of my boy," I tell her.

"A little? Dame, it was a hundred thousand deposited in my account."

"Let's just say I inherited the business."

"Oh . . . so what about me?" she asks as she walks to the bedroom. Trina is so damn sensuous and tempting, no straight man could ever turn her down. Trina sits on the bed and spreads her legs, revealing her pussy.

"You know I got you, ma."

"Come here, baby," Trina says as she starts playing with herself.

I'm gonna tear her ass up. Trina pulls off my clothes and I pull off her dress. I kiss her firm tits as she lies back on the bed. Ain't nothing like some good round-the-way pussy. I rub my dick up and down her slit, coating my dick head with her cum. I stroke her clit back and forth, enjoying the sensation.

"Ah . . . put it in, baby . . . stop playing with me."

I ram my dick between her legs and start to dig her out with some hard, short strokes.

"That's it, Dame . . ." Trina says as she lifts her torso, throwing that pussy at me. That's the one thing I love about Trina—she doesn't just like to lie there and let me do all the work. She likes to work it back. Trina keeps her thick legs spread wide as my dick stabs her creamy pussy.

"You got me cumming so much," Trina says. I ain't trying to brag, but a nigga does have a big dick. I make sure it presses up against her clit with every thrust.

"I want it doggy style!" Trina demands.

I pull out of her and see my dick covered with her white, milky cum. Trina turns around and I stare at that little fat ass of hers, then I slide it back in her pussy. Her pussy is so tight. All I can hear while my dick pumps is the sound of her juice coating my dick. I grab her ass cheeks and give her long, hard strokes, tapping all the sides. I'm bangin' her ass for a good 20 minutes non-stop.

"Shit, baby." I feel my nut coming.

"Don't stop!" Trina yells. It's time to give Trina my version of *The Fast and the Furious*. I start to bang her pussy so rapidly I'm like a blur. The room is filled with the sound of her ass slapping against my six-pack and Trina moaning at the top of her lungs. I finally bust a huge nut up in her.

"Oh, shit! Ahhh . . . fuck!" I ain't gonna front; I must've had a real ugly face on after that shit. I lean over on her ass and shudder from how good my dick feels inside of her warm pussy. Afterward, Trina and I lie in bed together, talking about my new position.

"So, what do you plan on doing now?" she asks me.

"What I always do. I'm gonna run this city."

"Dame, you're a fucking multi-millionaire now. You can't be on the block like a hustler anymore," she says.

"Why not?"

"Dame, how do you think the government got Al Capone? Tax evasion. You buying all this shit with no legit job to show for it is gonna be a big sign," Trina says. She is smarter than most chicks I mess with. That's why I like to talk to her about shit.

"King had those spas in Manhattan that he laundered money through."

"Yeah, a business you can put the money through. Besides, you gotta think of Taye's education."

"Don't worry about that. I'm gonna take care of my seed."

The more I think about it, the more Trina's words make sense to me. That was the reason King had invested in those spas. At first, I thought that was some weird shit, but now I see why he did it. The game ain't the same anymore between the NYPD, ATF, and IRS all cracking down on niggas. It's not like a nigga really needs to hustle anymore. Trina's right; I'm a fucking multi-millionaire now. The only reason we hustle is to get rich, and I ain't a greedy nigga, but

I do need something I can funnel this money through. After I let Harper's ass get so close to me, I know this shit can be taken away just like that. I really did trust that nigga, too. For now, I'm gonna have to let all these little roaches and rats here in New York know that just because King's dead doesn't mean the streets are open again. I run this shit.

A month goes by and Rob, Horse, and I have the streets on lock. The same way we ran things when King was alive is how we run shit now. I'm still trying to think of a legit way to put this money through. Like I said before, Rob is a smart nigga and knows how to handle himself. He takes me to this Amar Studio in East New York to see his boy Rodney Reid, a.k.a. Kane.

"Yo, I'm telling you, son, Kane is nice," Rob tells me.

"How you know this nigga?"

"When I was in Rikers, he was there doing a bid too."

"So why do you want me to meet him?" I ask.

"Because you have been saying you wanna find something legit to invest your money in, and I think he may be it," Rob replies.

"Well, he had better be fucking amazing."

We go in the studio and see Kane in the booth. This nigga is spitting with a mad flow. Rob wasn't exaggerating when he said that this nigga was nice. Now I see why Rob wanted me to meet this dude. This nigga has sick rhymes:

If I can't make money with you/ then fuck you/ that was code that niggas would roll to/ I decided if I couldn't get work/ figure I'll take work/ do whatever for the dollar/ put hot slugs in ya/ make you holla/ got your girl poppin' her pussy for a dollar-dollar/ a nigga so cool like the Fonz/ poppin' my collar/ You niggas know how I do shit/ got rappers retiring because how I run shit/ hoes be thinking/ that they'll have K trickin'/ No/ That nigga Kane be flippin'/ them model hoes he pimpin'/ I fuck 'em never love 'em/ they'll never catch me slippin'.

After he comes out of the booth, I sit and talk to him.

"What's up, Kane? This is my cousin Damien," Rob says.

"What's up, man?"

"What's up, son? You sound real nice," I tell him as I give him some dap.

"Thanks, I'm just doing what I do," Kane says.

"So, how long have you been trying to get in the game?"

"Man, I've been grinding for five years now, trying to get on, but all these fake-ass niggas at these record labels just want you to sound like the next nigga. I gotta be me," Kane says.

"I feel ya, nigga. You remind me of a thugged-out cross between DMX and Jay-Z. I like that shit."

"That's how we Harlem niggas get down. I heard you got Harlem on lock," Kane says to me as he sparks a blunt up.

"Like you said, I do what I do," I tell him.

"Word up, get that money, my nigga."

We end up talking about street shit for most of the night. Kane breaks out, and I give him my number. Rob was right about Kane being hot. Now I just want to figure out how we can make my dirty money clean.

"Yo, Rob, what's your plan? Ya boy's got talent, but how does that help me?" I ask him as we drive back to Harlem.

"I got a homie I went to school with called Tone who's A&R at Galaxy Records. I've been talking to him about Kane. Tone is making millions of dollars for them at Galaxy," Rob reveals.

"Yeah, so? What he saying?"

"I played him Kane's demo and homie was buggin' out, so I was thinking if we got behind Kane's project and promoted him on the streets, we could start our own record label with Tone. The record label is willing to cut him a check for five hundred thousand to do a joint venture with them."

"Really?"

"Yeah, man, we'll be our own record label and we'll distribute it through Galaxy Records."

"So you and Tone will run the business side, while I'll be a very silent partner."

"Exactly, my nigga. We can launder the money through the company and spend it legitimately."

So that's what we do. The following week I front the money so that Kane can press up 50,000 copies of his new mixtape and put them on the streets. Within two weeks we make sure every club is bumping his music. We put a copy of his mixtape in the hand of every major DJ from DJ Clue to Green Lantern and Kay Slay. Within a month, Kane is on everybody's mixtape. We flood the streets of Harlem, Brooklyn, Bronx, Staten Island and Queens with flyers advertising Kane's mixtapes. Every bodega and mom and pop record store has Kane's mixtape in it.

Pretty soon, major labels are hollering at my boy, but we have our connection with Tone at Galaxy. We call our label what else but Flip Set Records.

I'm so focused on getting this label off the ground that I let Horse run the corners. I still check in on him, but this was a way to make shit legit. I have to admit, drug money's nothing compared to this record industry money. The more I learn about it, the more I realize how much the record execs are ripping off these rappers. They some real corporate thugs, and pretty soon I'll be right there with them. The only thing that can stop my climb is the past, the shit I've done coming back to haunt me.

Horse calls me on my cell one night at the crib. "Yo, Dame, we gotta talk," Horse says urgently.

"What is it?"

"You remember that nigga Cornell you smoked a few months ago?"

"Yeah, what about him?"

"Looks like he was the little brother of that Jamaican nigga up in Brooklyn, Absolute," Horse says.

"Yeah, so?"

"Looks like that nigga found out it was you that hit him and word is that nigga is looking to get at you."

"Shit, a'ight, I'll meet up with you tomorrow at the spot on a Hundred forty-five Street."

"A'ight, one." Horse hangs up.

Damn, that's the last thing I need right now is some beef. Jamaican niggas are the wildest cats out here in New York. This nigga, Absolute, came from Kingston fifteen years ago and has most of Brooklyn on lock. Cornell was his half-brother or some shit. If this nigga wants to go to war with me, then I can handle him like any other roach. Problem being, with all this stuff starting to pop off with Kane, we don't need this kind of shit.

I just recently bought a house in upstate New York for Trina and Taye, a little four-bed-room place where I can rest my head. I don't want to buy a mansion and draw too much attention to us. I made sure the house was in Trina's name.

We continue to promote Kane's record in the streets and rent an office space on Lexington Avenue for Flip Set Records. In the meantime, we are at the studio recording Kane's debut LP.

A few weeks later we get the call from Tone at Galaxy saying that they want to do a joint venture with us. This is perfect. Everything is click-ing just right, so you know drama has to show up sooner or later.

I'm with Rob, Kane, Tone, and Horse at the office, talking shit and feeling happy that we got the deal with Galaxy.

"Didn't I tell you, nigga, this was going to pop off?" Rob says.

"You did, but if it wasn't for my nigga Kane, all this shit wouldn't be happening," I say to Kane.

"Man, you da one that blew a nigga up," Kane replies.

"Dog, when this album drops next month, we gonna really be killing these industry niggas," Tone says as we drink some Hpnotiq.

"Yo, Dame, what you gonna do about the corner store?" Horse mentions to me, referring to the game.

"My nigga, to be honest with you, I've been thinking of giving it up."

"What, you serious?" Horse says, surprised.

"Man, with all the money we gonna make off this music shit, there ain't gonna be no need to fuck with the corners anymore."

"I guess so."

"You know, my nigga, you rode with me through some ill shit. You a real solider, my nigga," I tell him.

"Yo, I'm a hood nigga. I'm down for anything at any time. These soft-ass niggas ain't ready for war, son," Horse says and knocks back his cup of Hpnotiq.

"It's time for a new hustle, my nigga. Kane is our number one investment now, so we gotta protect our assets. There's gonna be a few hat-ing-ass niggas out there."

"Don't worry about it. You know what they say: When it rains, niggas get wet," Horse says as he raises his shirt and shows me his .45 Magnum.

"That's my nigga," I say and give him a pound.

This shit makes sense to me. As much as I love the game, it's time to switch the hustle. Sure, I could continue to run the streets of Harlem, but it's only gonna be a matter of time before the feds come after me like they did King, or one of my workers flips on me like King flipped on my old man Bishop and I flipped on King. Besides, this music shit is ten times the amount of money we make on the streets. It's the right time to get out.

As we walk outta the office building, I see out the corner of my eye a car down the street that doesn't fit in. Here we are surround by Benzes, Lexuses, and Escalades, and there's a '94 Honda Civic parked down the street. I don't want to pull out and start blasting, but my instinct tells me something isn't right. As soon as we come through the lobby doors, I hear tires screeching and I know that this is a hit.

"Get down!" I yell as I duck down.

Budda, Budda, Budda, Budda!

Shots ring out from a semi-automatic sub-machine gun. We all scatter on the sidewalk and duck behind a parked truck in front of us. I pull out my Glock nine and bust six shots off at the car, but they bend the corner and haul ass. That nigga Absolute tried to mark me in broad daylight.

"Yo, Horse, get the car! We gonna kill these ma'fuckas for this shit!" I yell, but he doesn't answer me.

"Nigga, you deaf . . . ?" I turn around and see Horse shot the fuck up.

"Oh, shit." Horse has three to the chest and two in the head. A pool of blood is all over the sidewalk underneath him.

"Oh, fuck, he's dead!" Tone yells.

"Yo, Rob, I can't be here! I can't let the cops know I was here! Give me your keys!" I yell at him.

"Yo, get the fuck outta here." Rob throws me the keys and I take off for his car. I put the gun under my seat and head for a spot up in Harlem. I can't go home in case these ma'fuckas follow me.

This mutherfucka killed Horse and almost killed me! I can't believe I let this nigga catch me slipping. I shoulda seen this shit coming. I shoulda went after this nigga first as soon as I got the word.

Horse may have been a fat and ugly nigga, but he was still my nigga. He was probably the most reliable soldier on my team. I don't want to start any drama off that would fuck with this music business deal, but this nigga tried to take my whole crew out. I have to regroup, get my mind right, and figure out what my next move should be. This nigga Absolute wanna go to war, then fine. These ma'fuckas done turned me back into the old me.

16

The Omen

JANELLE

It's been six long months of recovery for Jayson and Nikki, and I've been here for both of them, but I haven't been doing it by myself. Quan has been right here with us. Jayson was able to keep Quan clear from being arrested 'cause he told them Quan quit dealing months ago. With King dead, Quan isn't really that important to them. Neither, I guess, is that asshole Damien. I still can't believe he's gotten away completely free after what he did to Nikki.

Quan has been staying with Jayson and me out in Decatur. He's buying a house down here for his mom and sister. He also filled out an application for Morehouse College and got a scholarship to go. His drive has motivated me so much that I got off my ass and got into the

University of Georgia. As much as things have
changed, I still feel like there's a part of Jayson
he keeps secret from me. I think his old commanding officer, John McNiven, feels the same
way too. He came by to visit Jayson at the house
today.

"So, how have you been feeling, Jayson?"
McNiven asks him.

"Better than I did six months ago," Jayson says
as he stands on a ladder to paint the outside of
the house. I'm holding the ladder for him.

"I see that. Jayson, I know that this was a very
difficult assignment for you, but are you sure
you don't wanna reconsider quitting the force?"

"I told you, John, I've had enough and I mean
it," Jayson replies.

"Hasn't Jayson put his life on the line enough
for you people?" I ask.

"Yes, he has, Janelle, and I'm happy that you
two found each other. I understand your reasons,
but I'm not talking about undercover work."

"Then what are you offering me, John? A desk
job filing reports? I don't think so," Jayson says
as he puts down another coat of tan paint on the
wall.

"No, not a desk job, but as a trainer for new
officers going undercover," McNiven says to him.

Jayson stops and looks at him. "Sounds interesting, but I'm not sure I'm the right man for the job. If you forgot, I got shot on my last assignment."

"No, I haven't forgotten, but you also infiltrated one of the deadliest gangs in the country for seven months and took down Dwayne 'King' Smith, a man the FBI was trying to get for over ten years. You can give these new undercover officers the insight they may need to keep themselves alive when they're in deep cover." McNiven lays it on thick for Jayson, and I can see that Jayson is thinking about it.

"I don't know, John. I need some more time," Jayson says.

"I'm not trying to rush you, Jayson. Take all the time you need. I just want you to know that we can use a man like you still. More importantly, those young cops can use a man with your experience. Well, I'll let you get back to work here. Take care, Janelle. Call me, Jayson." McNiven walks to his car and then drives off.

Jayson and I continue to paint the house and I decide to add my two cents.

"You know, I hate to admit it, Jayson, but he does have a point. You are the best at what you do, baby."

"No, I'm not. If I were I wouldn't have . . . I wouldn't have gotten shot," Jayson says, but I can tell he wants to say more. Jayson climbs down from the ladder. "I'm happy now. I got you in my life and I'm starting over."

"I'm glad you're with me, too, but I also know you're not that happy being here all day. I know you, Jayson. I know there are still some unresolved things you want answers to," I say to him.

"Like what?"

"Like where's Damien? And . . . what happened to Vanessa?" I say to him, and Jayson gets a sad look on his face.

"I couldn't care less about Damien. Sooner or later somebody is gonna put a couple of holes in him. And as far as Vanessa, I guess she got what she really wanted from all of this," Jayson says and then walks back to the garage.

I wish I knew what that was. As much as Jayson loves me, and I know he does, there's always a part of him that will also love Vanessa, whether he admits it to me or not. Why do I feel like there is a cloud that's hanging over us that we just can't shake?

DAMIEN

"We gonna kill this mutherfucka," I say to my homie, Irv Watts. Irv is a thoroughbred nigga I came up with from Spanish Harlem. He was up in Brooklyn running shit for King while I was in Atlanta. It used to be Irv, Nard, and me that ran together when we were just young niggas hustling. Nard got killed back in '96, God bless the dead.

"Whatever you need, I got ya," Irv says to me. It's been two weeks since Absolute's niggas shot Horse. I have to beef up my squad to handle this ma'fucka.

"Yo, that nigga Absolute is a grimy-ass nigga up in Brooklyn. This cat has been shooting up niggas left and right."

"Well, he made one mistake: he shoulda killed me the first time."

"So, what you wanna do? I know the hood they be hustling at. We can fuck them up right now," Irv says.

"Naw, I ain't doing any drive-by shit. I'm gonna catch this nigga slipping and do the shit myself. Besides, for right now I got 5-0 watching us too close."

These fucking hip-hop police are keeping tabs on Kane. After everything that went down at the office, the police really started to poke around and look at us. Horse, being a dead ex-con associating with industry cats, didn't sit right with the cops. I decide to keep a low profile and keep out of the limelight. Plus, I still had to deal with Absolute.

The funny thing is, the shooting only helped make Kane even more popular. The media thought that the hit was on him. Every music magazine put Kane on the cover. It's funny that I've been a hustler all my life and nobody ever put me on the cover of a magazine, but a rapper with a hot song and a shooting incident that didn't directly involve him could blow a nigga up.

Speaking of having a hot song, Kane's first official single, "Get Down or Lay Down," is blowing up on the charts. He has the number one single on the Billboard Top 100 and is the most anticipated new artist of the year. Kane also put out a dis track called "The Omen" from me to Absolute:

A prophecy/ for those who dare come test me/ listen carefully and you'll hear the truth/ Absolute power corrupts Absolute/ sending niggas for me that can't aim or shoot/ niggas wanna see me burn in hell/ like the devil's son did Cornell/ Flip Set runs shit/ kill any faggot nigga who wanna come get it.

Only niggas in the street that can read between the lines know what that song's about; they be going crazy when that shit hit. It's basically my declaration of war on Absolute.

Kane's album, *Hustlin' by Any Means Necessary,* becomes the top-selling album of the year according to the Billboard charts, moving in excess of 785,000 copies in its first week. SoundScan figures show that it's the third best-selling debut album in their history. Within a month, *Hustlin'* is double platinum, and Flip Set Records is the hottest record label in the game.

The six-figure checks from the ASCAP is more money than we can count. This is beyond what we coulda hoped for. I'm able to start laundering cash through the label just like we planned. This is the life: money, bitches, and weed. When we step up in the club, VIP is cleared out and only we're allowed to say who gets in.

This one night, we're in the 40/40 Club and Kane brings this bad-ass half Dominican and black chick named Beata up to VIP section. She's a video chick that Kane says he grew up with back in the day. He's been wanting to hit that shit for a long time now.

"Yo, this is my girl, Beata," Kane says to Rob and me.

"What's up, ma?"

"Hello," Beata says with a sexy-ass smile.

"You were the lead girl in Ne-Yo's new video," Rob says.

"Yeah, we shot that last month," Beata replies.

"So, how long have you known my man for?" I ask her.

"Oh, Kane and I go back," she says.

"Yeah, Beata has been playing hard to get for a minute now," Kane says as if he's hinting to something else.

"Well, a girl can't be too easy, right?" she says apologetically.

"I guess not."

Beata is a stallion for real. She reminds me of Mo'Nique back in Atlanta. I never did get to hit that ass. That's the one thing I do regret.

Kane and Beata leave the 40/40 Club together, and I can tell Kane wants to do more than just fuck this chick. Kane has a look on his face that says he and Beata had a lot of history between them. At any rate, it gave Rob and me a chance to talk about the situation with the cops and Absolute.

"Yo, Dame, you know five-o are watching us twenty-four/seven now since Horse got smoked," Rob says.

"I know. I can't afford to be connected to the shooting. I still got to deal with Absolute's bitch ass."

"We will, and with Kane selling all these albums, we ain't gonna have to worry about money. Yo, Kane even got Hollywood niggas sending him movie scripts," Rob tells me.

"Word? Let's get that money, my nigga."

Things are lovely. Rob and I are getting piss drunk on Moët that night. The next day, I go to the Flip Set offices in Manhattan, and while we're inside talking business, the NYPD raids our offices with a warrant.

"Get down! Hands where I can see them!" one pig yells as he shoves a gun in my face.

"Chill out, dude. Be easy," I say as they hand-cuff me.

"You have the right to remain silent. . . ." Another officer reads us our so-called rights.

All they find is a little bit of weed and a gun that's registered in Tone's name. They still take Rob and me downtown. They don't have shit on us. They take a bunch of financial records and try to charge us with money laundering. Too bad they can't prove shit. Everything we do is strictly off the books. Unfortunately, the van to central processing has already left for the night. That means spending overnight in the tombs. We would have to be arraigned in the morning.

After we see the judge, we're posted bond for $50,000 each, and the faggot-ass prosecutor is pissed they can't hold us on anything.

After that, I keep my distance from the label for about a month and avoid the cops, who fol-low me everywhere. At the same time, I have to keep my eyes open in case Absolute tries to hit me again. My nigga Irv is keeping tabs on that nigga Absolute, and finds out the spot where he's staying.

"Yo, my nigga, Absolute is staying up in Bed-Stuy, but he's got a fuckin' army surrounding him," Irv tells me.

"Where else nigga be going?"

"He fucks with some ho over on Flatbush Avenue."

"Does he? You know who the bitch is?" I ask him.

"No, but I can find out."

That's all I need to know. It's about time for me to show Absolute exactly who he's fucking with. In the meantime, I have to tighten up my circle and make sure these fucking cops can't build a real case against me. I'm pretty sure that since Tommy was a cop, they've had me under surveillance for a while. Although I wasn't the focus of their investigation, I was the number two man in King's operation. If they had any concrete evidence against me, they woulda come and got me.

The police decide to leave us alone for a minute since they can't find any evidence that would hold up in court. Kane is still at the top of the Billboard charts. We decide to keep the momentum going and push his next single.

We're shooting a video at a warehouse studio for Kane's next single, "Groupie Love," and I see Beata on the set. Kane tells me how he did ma dirty, and I bust out laughing. That's just what she deserves, but she's still fine. Word in the industry is that Beata done fucked a lot of industry niggas. I might as well be added to the list.

"What's up, ma?" I say as I walk up to her.

"Hey, what's up. You're Dame, right?" Beata says to me with that same sexy smile. She has on a short white miniskirt that barely covers that round, bubble ass. The front of the dress is a low halter-top that shows off her nice, golden brown tittes. My dick gets hard just staring at her fine ass.

"You remember me?" I ask her jokingly.

"Of course I do. I never forget a handsome face," Beata says flirtatiously.

"So, you here to see Kane?"

"Kane . . . no. I don't fuck with him anymore," she says firmly.

I bet you don't after how my nigga ran up in ya.

"I'm sorry to hear about that, ma."

"It's cool. Some niggas don't know how to treat a lady."

"So, why you here?" I ask her.

"I'm here to support my girl over there." Beata points to one of the girls on the set.

"Okay, cool. So what you getting into after this?"

"Nothing much," she says to me, smiling.

"You wanna ride with me?" I say as I put my arm around her waist.

"Sure. That's fine with me."

Ma is real cool. We drive to a beach in my S500 and we talk for a while. I ask her about what happened between her and Kane, and she tells me the edited version of how he dissed her. She also tells me that she can sing.

I ask her to sing a little something for me and she sings a little bit of Monica's "Angel of Mine." I'm surprised because ma can really sing. I tell her that I'll let her audition for Tone and Rob and try to get her signed to Flip Set Records. Ma has the look and the voice. She could make us a lot of money.

After a few minutes I decide to see how good her head skills are too. I pull out my dick and place my hand on the back of her head as ma slobs me down. Kane is right; ma can suck a mean dick.

After a minute or so I want some pussy, and she lets me hit it from behind in the back seat of the car. The pussy is just as good as Kane said it was.

She gives me her number, and I really do hook her up with Tone and Rob. Beata may be a gold digger, but at least we can pimp her ass with a record deal. We are looking for an R&B act, and she's perfect. Hoes need to eat too.

Irv is still trying to find out which bitch Absolute is fucking with on Flatbush Avenue. We are driving down the street, and we spot the nigga going into a Chinese restaurant on 129th Street.

"Yo, is dat Absolute's bitch ass?" I ask Irv.

"Hell yeah."

"Yo, Irv, pull over."

Irv pulls the car over.

"This nigga is by himself too."

"Yo, you wanna blast that nigga?" Irv asks me.

"Naw, I don't wanna draw too much attention to us. You still got that wood in the trunk?"

"Yeah, I do," Irv says.

We jump outta the car and Irv pops the trunk. We grab a pair of baseball bats and pull on some ski masks. We run up in the restaurant and start swinging on that nigga. He doesn't even see us coming. I bust that nigga upside the head. Absolute yells in pain. He tries to pull out his gat, but I smash his hand and the gun flies away.

"You tried to shoot me, nigga! Do something now!" I bust him again in the head.

Irv and me are having batting practice on this fool. I crack that nigga again in the face and break his jaw. One of the people from the restaurant starts yelling in that Chinese shit.

"How dat wood feel, nigga?" I yell as I break his arm. I think Irv fractures his legs.

"Come on, let's go!" Irv yells.

We hop in the whip and pull out. Absolute is lying in a bloodied, twisted mess on the sidewalk. We did that nigga old school style like my pops, Bishop, used to do. The last I heard, that nigga was in a wheelchair, eating from a tube. You don't always have to kill a nigga to set an example.

17

Life After Death

Atlanta, GA
One year later

JAYSON

I should be dead now. By all rights I should be, after being so stupid and trusting Vanessa. Lucky for me, somebody called the police after they heard shots. I woke up in the hospital a day later, and Janelle was right by my side. Poor girl had to deal with Nikki and me being laid up in critical condition at the same time. The whole situation was my fault. I should have never let Vanessa cloud my judgment like that.

After I was put in stable condition, I gave Lt. McNiven my final report. I don't know why, maybe my pride, but I never told him about Vanessa.

Vanessa and Damien set me up real good and put the gun that shot King in my hand. So, instead of telling him what really happened, I just let him believe what the evidence showed, that King found out I was an undercover cop, I pulled out, and we shot each other. The deal never went down. The police got rid of a major drug lord they couldn't touch, the D.A. got a promotion, and I retired from the force a month later.

The police raided and shut down most of the spots Damien had set up in College Park and East Point. Dre was also arrested and did a year in jail. Damien pulled up and left town before the cops could get to him. He wasn't the main focus of the D.A., and he wasn't a priority for them. If only they knew.

The only person that I personally looked out for was Quan. I felt like he was there for me and he was just caught up in a bad situation. A few months later, I helped him move his mom and little sister down from New York to Atlanta. He even enrolled in college at Morehouse and started to major in journalism.

I didn't even tell Janelle about what Vanessa did to me. I don't know why, but it really didn't seem important. I was alive, Vanessa was gone, and we could start our lives over again together.

I did, however, keep track of Damien. I had contacts on the force that let me know when Damien had returned to Harlem. Apparently he was keeping a real low profile.

A few months later, I saw a rapper called Kane on BET claiming he was a new artist on Flip Set Records. No doubt in my mind Damien was fronting the money for the label and probably laundering his fortune through it. I had to admit, it was a smart idea.

Janelle has begun to go to the University of Georgia, so we've decided to stay in Decatur. Lt. McNiven convinced me four months ago to come back and become an instructor on the force for undercover cops. I can't believe how green some of these rookies are. They have no idea how dangerous their world is about to become. It's my job to make sure they learn that, even though I'm not sure sometimes if I'm the best example for them.

Two days ago, I went to work and it was business as usual. A friend of mine was running a background check on some suspects. When he got up to get some lunch, I ran Vanessa's name through the country database on known gang associates, and I got an address for her in Los Angeles. Apparently her name was still on the FBI files of people known to be associated with Dwayne "King" Smith.

A million thoughts ran through my head as I stared at the address. She played me like a fool and tried to kill me. What was I gonna do, though? It's not like I could charge her with attempted murder, seeing how I didn't tell the complete truth about what happened that night. But I couldn't just let it go, either. You know what they say about karma. I think Vanessa is going to be reminded about that real soon.

JANELLE

It's funny how much changes in a year and a half. I'm now a sophomore at the University of Georgia. Just two years ago I was a stripper, doing almost anything for a dollar, lying to myself that this was the best hustle and that it was all I wanted to do with my life. That was until I met Jayson and he literally changed my life. Even though he was an undercover cop called Tommy, he still stole my heart. I feel like if he didn't enter my life when he did, I would still be dancing at The Pink Palace or worse.

After living through what Damien did to Nikki, it changed her life, too. She quit dancing.

I meet Nikki for lunch midtown at the Varsity, and we get a table.

"Girl, classes are gonna kill me this semester. I can't believe I got myself into this."

"I'm so proud of you, Mo," Nikki says.

"I ain't done nothing special."

"Girl, I've seen you grow from a little girl into a young woman, a college student at that. You still have that hustler's ambition, but only this time it's about getting that education. Looking back on it now, I should've pushed you to go to college in the first place instead of getting you into the game."

"Nikki, you took care of me the best way you knew how. Before you took me in, I was partially living on da streets. In case you forgot, you're not dancing anymore either."

"It took getting my ass kicked for me to learn," Nikki says regretfully.

"Don't even think about that, Nikki."

"I try not to, but . . . it's like I still got all this anger inside. He fucking raped me, beat me, degraded me, and got away with that shit," Nikki says sadly.

"I'm so sorry you had to go through that alone, Nikki," I say to her.

"Mo, you tried to warn me but I didn't listen. Now I just wanna . . . kill him."

I take her hand and wish I could take her pain away. "You're alive, Nikki. No matter what he did to you, you were stronger than that shit."

"If you say so."

We finish having lunch and I leave for class. Since Jayson and I have been so busy with work and school, it feels like we've barely been able to see each other. Being in class still feels so surreal. I used to think that college wasn't meant for me, but that was then and this is now.

Even now my past still has a way of showing up again. As I'm walking on campus, I run into somebody I haven't seen, or thought I would ever see again. My stepbrother, Tony.

"Janelle?"

"Oh my God, Tony." Even after five years his face still hasn't changed that much. "How are you, Tony?"

"I'm good. Damn, Janelle, I never thought I would run into you here."

"I never thought I would be here myself. So you've grown up a lot since the last time I've seen you."

"You too. After you broke out, I didn't stay at the house much longer either," Tony says. He gets an awkward look on his face when he says that to me.

"Listen, Janelle, I know what my dad did to you, and I'm sorry. I just didn't think my dad would be that kinda dude. I'm so sorry he hurt you."

"You don't have to apologize, Tony. You didn't do anything wrong. When did you leave home?" I ask him.

"About a year after you did. Pops started hitting the bottle even harder after you left. Then he started hitting me. I moved in with my aunt in College Park."

"Damn. So do you still see James anymore?"

"Every now and then. You ain't heard?"

"Heard what?"

"Pops ended up drinking so much that he developed cirrhosis of the liver."

"What?" I say, shocked.

"Yeah, Pops got diagnosed with it three years ago and has been bed-ridden for a year now."

Whoa, I don't know whether I should be happy or sad for the old man. I know it's cold, but that's what that bitch deserves.

I stay and talk to Tony for a few more minutes before he ends up going to class. It's good to see him again, and we exchange numbers. Before he leaves, Tony tells me that James is still staying in the same house in Bankhead.

I haven't been back to Bankhead since I left five years ago. Part of me never wants to go back there, especially after what he did to me, but since I've been able to turn my life around, I do wanna see him again. I wanna show that son of a bitch that I survived and that he doesn't intimidate me anymore. I want him to know that he took a part of my life away.

For the rest of the day, all I can do is remember all those painful feelings I've been carrying around for the past five years.

After class, I find myself driving to Bankhead instead of going home. I guess I have to see him for myself. As I pull into my old neighborhood, it looks pretty much the same. It's one of the few spots in Bankhead that isn't ghetto as hell.

I pull into the driveway and walk to the front door. I just stand there for a moment, frozen in my tracks. I guess I'm debating to myself if I really want to go through with this or not.

"Hello, may I help you?" The door opens unexpectedly, and standing there is a white woman dressed in medical scrubs.

"Ah, yeah. I was here to see James Steffen. I'm his stepdaughter, Janelle."

"Oh, Janelle. I've heard James talk about you. Come in. I'm Debra, his home health aide," she says, smiling as she lets me in.

"He has talked about me?" I ask, surprised.

"Yeah, you and Tony. I don't think he thought you would come see him after the fight you two had."

"Fight?" I ask, confused.

"Yeah, he said you moved away from home after that day."

"Oh." *So that's the story he tells people now.* "So, how is he?"

"Not too good. He's lost a lot of weight because of his illness." We walk to his room. "I'll give you two some privacy."

Debra walks to the living room, and I glance down the hall to my old bedroom. The memories of what he did to me come back. I build up all the courage I can muster and open his door.

When I see James, I'm shocked. When Debra said he lost weight I had no idea she meant this much. The last I saw James he was at least 250 pounds. Now he looks like he's 125 at the most. His skin and fingertips are yellowish. He sleeps soundly, unaware that I'm in the room.

I guess that he senses someone is there with him because he opens his eyes and looks at me.

"Oh my God, Janelle," he says with a weak voice. Even James' eyes and teeth are yellowish. He looks like a zombie. He really is on his death-bed.

"Yeah, it's me," I say to him, trying to hold back the anger I feel.

"I never thought I would you see you again. How have you been?" he asks me.

"Fine."

"I'm glad you came. I've been worried about you . . . since you left home. After your mother passed . . . I promised her I would look after you. I guess I should have looked after myself, too. I'm sorry for what happened between us. I was drunk, but that's no excuse. I'm just glad you came here. I'm glad you found it in your heart to forgive me before I died."

I can't believe what I heard this nigga just say. I lose what little self-control I have. "Forgive you? You think I came here to forgive you? After what you did to me, after what my life has been like since then? I didn't come here to forgive you. I just came here to make sure you were dying, nigga. I hate your fucking guts. You stole my innocence. You fucking raped me!"

"You can't mean that, Janelle." James has on a look of dismay.

I walk up to him and get in his face. He smells like a pharmacy because of all the medication he's on. James gets a look of fear 'cause he realizes the roles have reversed and that I'm the one in power now.

"It would be so easy to kill you, but you deserve to live the rest of your short, meaningless last days like this. I just want you to know that you didn't ruin my life no matter what you did to me. Rest in peace, muthafucka." I turn and walk out of his room.

Now, I know God says to forgive, but some things are too hurtful to let go. Like I said, karma is a bitch. Truth be told, I had half a mind to put a pillow over his face and kill him, but after seeing him like that, killing him would be doing him a favor.

I walk by Debra in the living room.

"You're leaving so soon?"

"Yeah."

"Whatever it was that happened between you two, it's time to let it go. Life is too short to hold on to grudges," she says to me.

"He raped me when I was sixteen years old."

Debra is shocked. "Oh my . . ."

"He deserves everything he's going through," I say to Debra as I walk out the door.

I drive home feeling good about what happened. It wasn't really revenge; it was more like closure to the most horrible event in my life.

When I get home, Jayson is in the den on the computer.

"Hey, baby," I say.

"Hey."

"Whatcha working on?" I ask him as I hug him around the neck.

"Just some reports I have to finish," Jayson says.

I look on the desk and see a file that has Vanessa's name on it. "Why do you have that file, Jayson?"

"I was just doing a follow-up on some things."

I stand up and Jayson turns and looks at me as I walk away.

"Janelle . . . Janelle, what's wrong?"

"What's wrong? Jayson, you don't think I know when you're lying to me?"

"Janelle . . ."

"Don't. If it's not the truth, I don't wanna hear it."

"Janelle, you're overreacting."

"To your having a file of your ex-drug-deal-er-dating girlfriend on your desk? Now why shouldn't I be upset?"

"Because . . . I'm trying to find her because . . ." Jayson pauses as if he has something else to say but can't.

"Because why, Jayson?"

"Because she's the one that shot me," Jayson says.

Okay, talk about a bombshell.

"Vanessa shot you and you didn't tell me?"

"At the time, you had gone through so much that I didn't want to upset you even more. It was finally over and Vanessa was long gone. I just wanted to put that all behind us. Plus, with the report I gave, the less you knew the better."

Now, the old me would be pissed the fuck off for him not telling me the truth, but I do see why he did it.

"Okay, I understand, sorta. I'm not happy about it, but I understand your reason. So, why do you have her file now?"

"I ran her name in the computer and found an address for her in L.A."

"Let me guess. You were going to pay her a little visit."

"Something like that. Do you have any ideas about what I should do when I see her?"

I get a devilish grin on my face. "Yeah, I do, as a matter of fact."

18

Ghetto Love

NIKKI

What happened to me a year and half ago was a reality check. I'm not saying I'm glad it happened, but it forced me to look at my life through clear eyes. The reality was that I was selling my body and my life to the nigga with the most money. I justified using what I got to get what I want to avoid facing the truth. I used to call the men I slept with tricks, but I was the one selling myself short. The day Damien and Horse raped and beat me showed me that I was just a piece of shit in their eyes. They thought that I was trash because I never respected myself enough to change my life.

Fortunately, I survived what they did to me, and that traumatic event finally caused me to change. Mo'Nique and Penny stood by my side and took care of me. It's funny, but the only other person that gave a damn about me was Dre.

Dre was irate after he found out what Damien did to me. It was right after Damien came through Bankhead and shot four of Dre's boys. I always kept Dre at a distance, never allowed myself to feel anything for him, or show it, but the truth was I did care about Dre.

Dre wanted to kill Damien more than I did, and he would have went to New York and murdered him if he didn't get locked up.

Dre has been in jail now for the past ten and a half months, and I've visited him twice a month since he's been in. He's scheduled to be released this Monday morning.

Since Dre's been in jail, I've quit dancing and started to work at a department store. Dre was happy when I told him I quit dancing, and he promised me that he was going to give up the game. I know it's easy to say things when you're locked up, but I feel like Dre meant what he said. Even though I know I shouldn't be involved with a thug, I can't help but have feelings for him.

I get a call from Dre on Sunday afternoon, the day before he is supposed to get out. The automated voice says, "Will you accept a collect call from Dre? If yes, please press one." I push the button and hear Dre's voice.

"Hey, baby, what's good?"

"What's good is that I'm going to be in your arms tomorrow morning," I say happily.

"I know. I can't wait to be with you, Nikki, but you know I have to report to my parole officer by one p.m. or they'll put out a warrant for me."

"That's all right. You'll be there way ahead of time."

"Well, you know we gonna have to stop at a hotel or something so I can get up in that sweet thing. I hope you can handle me, Nikki. A nigga is a little backed up, ya know."

"No doubt. So am I. You know I haven't been with another dude since . . . you know."

"Yeah, I know. I'm just sorry I wasn't able to catch up with that nigga. Nikki, you know since I've been in here, I've had to spend a lot of cash on my lawyer to get some of those charges dropped."

"Yeah, I know."

"I had no choice. A nigga was looking at a few years if I woulda rolled over."

"I know you would've. You told me."

"I'm just saying I don't have money like I used to, so if you don't wanna . . ."

"Dre, I done told you that money ain't as important to me like that anymore. I don't care if you are barefoot and homeless. I wanna be with you. After everything I've been through and all the lowdown shit I've done, you're the only man that's loved me just for me. I just wanna be with you."

"Damn, Nikki, you don't know how long I've wanted to hear you say that," Dre says gladly.

"And I'm gonna say that to you again tomorrow morning when I see you. I'll be there at six o'clock waiting for you, baby."

"I love you, Nikki."

"I love you too."

"So, I'll see you tomorrow."

"Okay, baby. Bye."

I hang up the phone and smile to myself, knowing that tomorrow I'll be with my man again.

Since I've been out of the game, I've still been in contact with Penny. I babysit her baby boy, Tarius, while she dances at The Pink Palace. I try to encourage her to get out, but I know how addicting the fast money can be. I know that if I didn't go through my drama with Damien and somebody tried to get me to quit dancing, I woulda paid them no attention.

Penny has Tarius to worry about too. It's not like she got a college degree and can go get a corporate job somewhere, so she's gotta do what she gotta do. Although I did get her to stop doing the private parties we used to do together. We used to run into all types of freaks in those parties—freaks with nasty little fetishes. No time for that shit.

I go to The Pink Palace to see Penny. She says that her mother isn't able to take care of Tarius and she needs me to pick him up from the club. I know this is the last place you should have your baby at. It's been about nine months since I last set foot in there, and it feels like the first time again. Sure, the same niggas are there, trying to get a girl to come home with them. Other than a few new girls, most of the regulars are still here, popping pussy on stage.

I feel like a new woman when I walk in the Palace, and for the first time ever I feel out of place in there. As I walk through the club some guy recognizes me and grabs my hand.

"Hey, Nikki, it's been a while since I seen your fine ass in here. You gonna work a little somethin' for me tonight?"

I pull my hand away. "No. I don't dance anymore, and don't put your hands on me again."

"Damn, bitch, it's like that?"

"Yeah, bitch, it's exactly like that. Besides, you wouldn't have been able to afford me when I was dancing." I walk away and go backstage and see Penny.

"Girl, I'm glad you came," Penny says to me.

"Yeah, you know I got you and my little man," I say as I pick up Tarius and Penny hands me his bag.

"He just ate, so he should be fine for the rest of the night."

"Okay. Penny, you know this ain't the right atmosphere for Tarius to be around, ya know? He's getting old enough to start learning things."

"I know, Nikki. I don't wanna bring him around this shit, but what choice do I got? I need money or we can't eat. If I had another option I would consider it."

"I know, girl. So you know you'll have to pick him up as soon as you get off tonight. Dre is coming home tomorrow morning."

"Damn, Nikki, I've never seen you so happy before."

"I know. I just feel like tomorrow is going to be a new beginning for us."

"I feel like that too."

I take Tarius home and put him to bed. All I can do is think about seeing Dre in the morning. I have already reserved a room a few blocks away from his parole officer's building at a place called the Doubletree Hotel.

Penny comes through at about 4 a.m. to pick Tarius up. That's okay because I'm already up and getting ready to go to the jailhouse to get Dre. I couldn't sleep most of the night anyway.

I leave the house at about 5:15 a.m., drive to the jail, and wait by the gates where he is going to be released. The next forty-five minutes seem like the longest time in the world to me. Then it finally turns six o'clock, and I get up out of my car and stare at the gate. About one minute later, I see Dre walking toward the gate. Just seeing him there makes my pussy get wet.

Dre is holding a brown paper bag with all of his personal belongings in it. As he walks past the gates, I move toward him. Finally I reach him and jump into his arms, giving him a passionate tongue kiss. Dre holds me in the air as I wrap my legs around his waist.

"I'm so happy to see you, baby," I say to him.

"Not half as happy as I am to see you," Dre replies.

We get in my car, drive to the hotel and check into our room. I have to admit that for the first time ever I feel nervous being with a man. Although all my physical wounds from the incident have long healed, I still have some mental shit about being with Dre again. I don't want to feel like that again.

I half expect Dre to rip my clothes off and take my ass right there on the floor, but he surprises me. I guess Dre can see how anxious I am once we get in the room. Dre kisses my lips and slowly undresses me. First he unbuttons my blouse and then undoes my bra. My titties pop out, and Dre cups them with his hands. Then he takes off his shirt, and I can tell by his muscular chest that Dre must have pumped iron every day he was in there. Then he undoes his pants and pulls down his underwear, and oh, man, it looks like his dick got bigger in there!

Dre is a sculpted Greek god standing there in front of me naked. From his perfectly formed six-pack and muscular arms, Dre could have easily been a male model. He undoes my jeans and pulls them down, and I stand there in my thong, oozing with excitement.

Dre picks me up and carries me to the bed and lays me down. This is a side of Dre I've never seen before. He spreads my legs and begins to lick my clit through my lace thong, adding to the moisture that's already there pooling up. Then he pulls it to the side and lets his tongue lick my clit back and forth, and I moan in pleasure. I can't believe this is Dre I'm with. He has never gone down on me like this before. All I can do is gyrate my hips up and down to match his tempo.

Dre slowly works his way up my stomach with baby kisses, until he reaches my breasts and licks my stiff nipples. Then he kisses me up my neck and begins to tongue kiss me. I can taste my juices on his lips as our tongues touch.

I don't know when he does it, but somewhere between licking and kissing me Dre is able to slip on a magnum-size condom. Then I feel his monster push up in my pussy, and I shudder from the size of it inside of me. I haven't had sex in a long time so I must be tight like a virgin again!

"Aaahhh . . ." I moan. I'm so wet that it went in with no problem.

Dre works the middle so deep that he bottoms me out with each stroke. Surprisingly, Dre isn't going crazy banging me out like he used to. Instead, he allows me to find my rhythm, and I move my hips up and down on his dick like I'm working an oversized dildo. I feel so good that I forget about last year's traumatic experience and just enjoy the moment.

Dre pulls out of me and rests with his knees on the bed. "You okay, Nikki?" Dre softly says to me.

"I've never felt better."

"Well, let me see if I can make you feel even better than that. Turn around."

For a second I have a flashback to what happened with Damien, but I turn around and bend over anyway, pushing that nightmare out of my mind. Dre takes two pillows and places them underneath my stomach so that I can be comfortable. He starts to rub my ass as if he were going to tear me up fo'sho! I brace myself and prepare for his gigantic dick to drill right through me.

Then he spreads my ass cheeks, and I tighten my stomach muscles, and then I feel a soft, thick tongue licking my pussy. Dre unleashes his "Tasmanian Devil Tongue" on my clit, and I'm blown. I've never had my pussy eaten in the doggy style position before. I swear Dre's tongue is everywhere from the bottom of my pussy to the clit and even over my ass. I can feel his whole face in me.

"Ooohmygodaaahhh! Ah! Aaaahh! Fuck!" I start moaning strange gibberish at the top of my lungs that makes no sense. I cum harder than I ever came in my life.

Dre must look like he just got done competing in a watermelon eating contest when he comes up from me. I turn my head back and look at him, and his face is glistening. I am so horny that now I want some more dick.

"Give me that dick, Dre."

Dre obeys and rams that hulking dick back into me and fucks me royally like the old Dre. Now he knows that I'm ready to handle all that backed-up tension he was feeling for the last ten months and releases the beast.

"Oh God . . . you're so deep," I cry out in ecstasy.

Dre tears my ass up for a good hour before pulling out, ripping the condom off, and putting himself back in to cum inside of me. Then he collapses on my back, and we lie on the bed, huffing and puffing. Dre holds me in his arms and we exchange sweet nothings to each other.

"I love you, Dre."

"I love you too, Nikki. I always have," Dre says.

"I know you did. I just didn't wanna believe any man could really be in love with me."

"Well, I am, and I'm not going anywhere."

I kiss Dre and we lay in bed for another two hours before we leave so that Dre can check in with his P.O.

19

Karma's a Bitch

JANELLE

This isn't about revenge. This is about justice. Okay, maybe a little revenge, too, because this bitch Vanessa did try to kill Jayson, but we'll have to do this on our own. Since Jayson never told the police about Vanessa's involvement, the bitch got a free ride out of town. He can't change his story now. Meanwhile, Jayson has been digging into what she's been doing for the past year and a half.

Every time I think about how Jayson and I met, it blows my mind to know that we're still together. We were two different people, literally, but somehow we both connected. I love Jayson and he loves me. We didn't know how this was going to work, us being together, but somehow we made it.

After Jayson got shot, I nursed him back to health and in return he gave me something real in my life, but even after all that I still feel like there's a part of Jayson that feels hurt by what happened. When I ask him what happened to Vanessa, he just tells me that she disappeared. In all honesty, I think that he's holding back the truth for my sake.

I pick up the phone to call Nikki and tell her what we just found out.

"Hey, cuz, you've been incognito for the past two weeks since Dre's been home."

"What's up, Mo? Girl, me and Dre have been making up for some lost time together."

"So I see. So I guess that means you're back in the saddle again," I playfully ask her.

"In the saddle? Mo, I've been riding Dre like the Kentucky Derby! Mo, I swear that he's gotten bigger and better since he's been in jail."

"What? It's like that?" I ask.

"Girl, let me put it to you this way: Dre has got the best head game I've ever had," Nikki exclaims happily.

"Damn, go 'head with ya bad self! I'm glad you're happy again, Nikki."

"For the first time in a long time, I truly am."

This is the first time I've seen Nikki happy with a man.

"So, what up, Mo?" Nikki asks.

"Well, I just found out some things from Jayson about what happened when he got shot."

"What happened?"

"You remember that bitch Vanessa?" I ask her.

"Yeah, I remember that ho. She dipped outta town as soon as her man got popped."

"Yeah, well, it turns out Jayson didn't tell the police what really happened. Vanessa was the one that shot him."

"What?"

"Yeah, and Jayson didn't kill King. It was Damien."

Nikki doesn't respond for a second.

"Are you all right, Nikki?"

"Yeah, I'm fine. Why didn't he have them both arrested?"

"It's a long story, but Vanessa was Jayson's ex-girlfriend in high school. She lied to him and said she was trapped by King and played on his feelings for her. Turns out her and Damien were running a game on King to get to his money. Damien killed King, and Vanessa shot Jayson. They made it look like they shot each other to death and dipped with the money. Only problem was Jayson wasn't dead."

"So why didn't Jayson bust them fuckers later?" Nikki asks, still confused.

"Jayson never told the police about his connection with Vanessa while he was undercover in the first place, and after it all went down, I think Jayson felt like . . . I don't know, like it was over and done with. I guess he didn't want to deal with it anymore."

I can tell Nikki's upset about Damien being free because Jayson never told. "So why did Jayson decide to tell you now?"

"Because we just found out where she's been for the past year and a half. She's been living out in L.A.," I tell her.

"So what are you going to do now?"

"I don't know yet, but I think Jayson might do something. Nikki, I'm sorry if this brings back too many painful memories for you."

"Mo, I'll be fine. I got Dre in my life now, but I hope Jayson doesn't let her get away with trying to kill him. I know he's a cop and everything, but that bitch has done too much shit to him."

"I know. I wanna see the bitch myself. I might catch a charge too when I'm done with her."

"Has he heard anything else about Damien?" Nikki asks.

"No, not lately, although he thinks that he's got something to do with that Flip Set Records up in New York."

"You mean he's behind that rapper Kane?"

"Maybe."

"I had a feeling that he was connected somehow. Nobody is just gonna claim the name Flip Set for the hell of it. I can't believe that nigga is still free, walking around spending millions after what he did to me," Nikki says angrily.

"Don't worry, Nikki. Sooner or later that nigga is gonna get dealt with. His type always does. With all the slime he's done to people, it's just a matter of time before somebody catches up with him."

"I know you're trying to make me feel better, but it still bothers me. Niggas like that shouldn't be allowed to live, walk, or reproduce!"

"I know what you mean. Nikki, I never told you this because at the time there was so much craziness going on, but . . ."

"What is it, Mo? Nothing can surprise me now," Nikki says.

"When I left the house back then it wasn't to go see Aunt Gene. It was because that night before, Damien tried to rape me in the living room."

"What? Mo'Nique, why didn't you tell me?"

"I'm sorry, Nikki, but he said if I told you he would kill you and me, and I didn't want to put you in danger. I guess that didn't work either, because look what happened. I always felt that if I had told you, maybe you would have never been atta—"

Nikki cuts me off.

"Mo—Janelle, what happened to me was in no way your fault. It was that pig. My God . . . how did you stop him?"

"I couldn't stop him. The only reason he didn't rape me was because you and Penny came home at the right time. You saved me and you didn't even know it. The next day, I told Jayson, and he got me out of town to his place in Savannah, but if I woulda known what would happen to you . . ."

"Janelle, there's no way you coulda known what that animal was gonna do."

Nikki and me continued to talk for another hour or so, until she had to go to work. It felt good getting that off my chest after all this time. Nikki is a lot stronger than Damien knew. I know he'll get his eventually, but for right now it's time to deal with this bitch Vanessa.

JAYSON

For the past few days I've been doing a background check on Vanessa, trying to find out what she's been doing for the past year. Apparently she bought a mansion out in L.A. and makes trips to the Cayman Islands quite frequently. As I dig a little deeper, I find out that Vanessa still has a connection to Atlanta.

Her name came up in some moving company records. Two years ago, Vanessa rented a Ryder truck to move some stuff down from New York to a storage building down in College Park. The storage unit has been paid up for three years, and whatever it holds has just been sitting there.

Janelle and I drive to the storage area down in College Park. I have a feeling Vanessa wasn't the one that paid off the storage unit for three years. Fortunately, I still have documents that I "borrowed" from King's office, along with a spare key. I find paperwork that has the name and address of the self-storage place.

"So, what do you think Vanessa had moved down here?" Janelle asks me.

"I don't think Vanessa even knew about this."

I open the storage unit, and we see moving boxes stacked from the floor to the ceiling.

"Wanna guess what's inside?"

"Only one way to find out." I take out a box cutter and break the tape seal on a box and open it.

"Oh, shit. It's like a Johnson & Johnson baby powder stockpile in here," Janelle says, stunned by bricks of cocaine.

"Just what I thought. King was using Vanessa to transport cocaine from N.Y. to College Park in her name. There's enough coke here to put her away for the next twenty years."

"So, what should we do now?" Janelle asks.
"Have you ever been to L.A.?"

Four days later, Janelle and I are on a flight to L.A. together. It's weird, because it's kinda like a vacation for us, but it's not. Our first trip together and we're plotting on taking down my ex-girlfriend. Not something every couple does, but I guess we're just weird like that.

I still think about that night and how easily Vanessa shot me in cold blood after everything we had been through. I guess I was a fool to believe that she was the same girl I knew back then.

We check into our hotel and rest after our flight. There is no need to rush this. Vanessa doesn't have any clue that I'm still alive or that she's a part of a drug trafficking operation.

"Janelle, we haven't talked about this much, but how do you feel?" I ask her.

"I don't know, Jayson. Weird, I guess. A part of me is happy we're about to do this, and another part of me still feels like I'm in competition with the girl from your past."

"Janelle, that's all she is to me now, a faded memory from my past. She's not the girl I knew back then. You're the woman I love now. Besides, when she shot me, it kinda killed any chance of us ever being together again."

"Thanks for reminding me about that. I can't wait to see her," Janelle says coldheartedly. Well, if a woman scorned is bad, I'm afraid to see how a woman that wants revenge is. They say payback is a bitch, and her name is Janelle.

The next day we find Vanessa's four-bedroom house in an upscale area. We stake out down the street until we see her leave in her silver BMW. I guess she's still living somewhat low-key. Then Janelle and I walk up to her house and to the back door.

"No alarm system, so this should be easy," I tell her. You learn a thing or two being a cop, including how to pick a lock. It takes about forty-five seconds and we're inside.

"Ain't this some shit," Janelle says as she walks inside and looks at her big-ass kitchen.

"This bitch has been living the life." This is a long way from growing up in the hood in Savannah.

I make my way to her study and look on her desk and see an airline ticket to the Caymans for tomorrow morning at eight a.m. I look around more and find deposit slips for a bank in the Caymans. Vanessa has deposited over twenty-four million into that account over the past year.

"Janelle, go check her bedroom and see if she has a suitcase packed already."

Janelle walks into her bedroom and finds two suitcases. "Jayson, come take a look at this."

I come in and Janelle has opened the small carry-on and finds an envelope with $10 million worth of savings bonds in it.

"Where is she going with so much cash?"

"She's been transferring money into her bank account in the Cayman Islands so the IRS can't find out. Come on, let's do what we're here to do."

Later that night, Vanessa comes home and walks in the front door. She throws down her jacket and walks into her study and turns on the lights.

"Oh my God!" Vanessa yells when she sees me sitting behind her desk.

"Yeah, I do seem to have that effect on people."

"Jayson, you're . . ."

"Alive? Not from a lack of trying on your part," I say to her.

"Jayson, I had no choice. Damien would've—"

"Would've what? Gone to prison? You had a choice, Vanessa; you just chose to kill me. You played me like a fiddle, and I fell for it."

We stare at each other for a few seconds in silence. The tension is so thick that I can feel the hairs on the back of my neck standing up.

"So, what are you here to do now, Jayson, arrest me?" Vanessa asks bluntly.

"No. I just wanna know why. Why, after everything we meant to each other, you would put a bullet in my gut."

Vanessa stares at me coldly, then answers me. "I told you, Jayson, I was going to share this all with you, but you chose that little stripper ho over me. I loved you, Jayson. I've been in love with you since the day we met in high school, but I wasn't going to let you or nobody stand in my way."

"At least you're honest about your shit. Were you fucking Damien too?"

"Hell no. We had a business arrangement. And since you obviously didn't tell your bosses about what really happened that night, you can't prove anything. So why are you here?" Vanessa asks me.

"Well, you know what you said to me about a woman scorned?"

"Yeah, I do. So?" she says sarcastically.

Janelle walks in behind Vanessa. Her eyes are filled with fury and her fists are clenched.

"Remember me, bitch?" Janelle says to her.

Vanessa turns around and sees her. "What the hell are you doing—" But before Vanessa can finish her sentence, Janelle hammers her with a haymaker across the jaw. Vanessa is taken completely off guard by her punch and falls flat on the ground. Janelle takes advantage and grabs her by the collar.

"That was for trying to kill my man." Janelle then pimp-slaps her in the mouth. "That was for calling me a ho, bitch!" Janelle yells at her.

Vanessa tries to push her off, but Janelle is too strong for her as she grabs her arm and flips her on her back and twists her arm.

"Aarrgh!" Vanessa yells in pain.

"I should break this muthafucka off right now, bitch!"

"Janelle . . . that's enough. Let's go."

"You're lucky that it wasn't just me who came here tonight, bitch." Janelle lets her go, and we walk out.

Vanessa wipes the blood from her lip. She jumps up and grabs the Glock 19 from her desk and points it at us.

"I'm gonna kill you both!" Vanessa yells.

"It wouldn't be the first time you tried. But could you do it again?" I ask her.

"I have no problem with that." Vanessa pulls the trigger. *Click, click.*

"You really think I'd let you shoot me again? Think again. Good-bye, Vanessa." We walk out the door.

"Fuck you both! I swear you're going to regret this shit!" Vanessa yells.

"Feel better?" I ask Janelle.

"Much better."

The next morning, Vanessa leaves for the airport at 5:30 a.m. to catch her flight to the Cayman Islands. She wears a pair of aviator shades to cover up the black eye Janelle gave her. Vanessa is right about one thing—I had no evidence against her. But that doesn't mean she's going to go free. When she goes through airport security, they X-ray her bag and find a brick of cocaine in her suitcase. They also find ten million in savings bonds. Officials charge her with international drug trafficking. I then turn over evidence to the local ATF from the storge unit filled with cocaine in College Park. Vanessa is looking at federal time.

Janelle and I return to Atlanta the same day. Our plan went down as smoothly as possible. This wasn't about revenge, or I just would've shot her. This was about justice. Okay, perhaps a little revenge. She did shoot me, after all. Like they say, karma's a bitch.

20

Who Shot Ya?

JANELLE

It's been two months since we came back from L.A. and dealt with Vanessa's trifling ass. Jayson has to fly back out there to present more evidence against her for the prosecution. She's now facing international drug trafficking and money laundering charges. She should be locked up for the next twenty to thirty years. The media is calling this the biggest drug bust in Fulton County history and calling Vanessa the queen behind King's New York operation. They gonna throw her ass up under the jailhouse!

I'm just happy that ho got what she deserved. As for me, it's time to concentrate on graduating next month and getting my A.S. degree. The University of Georgia ain't no joke when it comes to exam time. Now that I'm about to finish my general ed classes, I'm thinking about what major I should decide on. I thought about becoming a teacher for a hot second, until I remembered how much I didn't enjoy high school. The nursing field is pretty wide open. I do like working and taking care of newborns, so that's definitely a possibility. For now, I had better focus on passing this physics exam I got next Tuesday.

There are a lot of things jumping off in the A-town, and some concerts that are going on at the school. As I'm leaving class, there's a crowd of people gathered outside the auditorium, and I see my stepbrother, Tony.

"Hey, what's up, Tony?"

"Hey, Janelle. Nothing much, man," Tony says.

"What's all the commotion for?"

"Don't you know? Kane is signing autographs before he performs."

"Kane? The rapper?" I ask.

"Yeah, I'm just trying to get some of his groupie leftovers for myself."

All of a sudden I get a bad feeling in my gut. "Tony, I gotta go."

"Okay, I'll holla at ya."

I start to walk away from the crowd and push past people in my way. I know I might be bugging out a little, but I'd rather be safe than sorry.

As I'm making my way down the block, my worst fears come face to face with me again.

"Hey, ma, long time no see," Damien says.

My heart starts to beat rapidly and I wanna run away, but I can't. Damien stares at me with those lustful eyes.

"Damn, you still look finer than a bitch."

"I gotta go," I say to him as I try to walk by him, but he grabs my arm.

"Where you running off to so soon? We just gonna catch up on some old times."

"We don't have anything to catch up on. Let me go," I demand.

"Don't act like that, Mo. Let's just get to know each other again."

"Let go of me or I'll scream!"

"Now, why would you wanna go and do that, ma?" Damien says as he shows me his gun under his shirt. "Now, how's life been treating you? You going to school? Shit, got your life all together now. I just wanna finish what we started back in the day."

"You mean rape me like you did Nikki?"

Damien looks at me coldly. "Naw, I ain't gonna rape you. I'm gonna fuck you. And you're going be cool with it, or I'll have to look up that ho-ass cousin of yours again. You feel me?"

I won't let him hurt Nikki again, not after what happened the first time. Jayson's not here, and I can't run away from him again.

"Okay. Just let me go home and change," I say to him.

"Naw, ma, I like the way you look right now. We can go somewhere real private." Damien lets go of me and points to his car. We get in and we pull off down the street.

"That's my nigga, Kane, back there. I put him on. I'm making a lot of big moves in the rap game, ma. A girl like you could make some real paper in the game with an ass like that. Of course you need the right man behind you to make it happen."

I don't respond. All I can do is think of how I let myself get caught by this nigga.

"Well, I guess I'm gonna get behind that ass of yours one way or another. Tell me, did you go to that bitch-ass Officer Harper's funeral?" Damien says.

Oh my God, he thinks Jayson is dead. No need to tell him shit.

"I don't wanna talk about him."

"That nigga really had you sprung, huh? He's probably the reason you quit dancing and shit. You really thought he was Captain-Save-a-Ho?

That nigga fooled me, too. You see, the truth is, Mo'Nique, bitches like you are only good for fucking. All this college shit just ain't you. You were better off making your ass clap back in The Pink Palace. Just remember that."

Damien drives me to a shitty little Days Inn on the west side of Atlanta and checks us in. It's a small room with a king-sized bed, two nightstands, and a dresser with a TV on it. Damien is still the same asshole he was back then, except this time he has more money. By the platinum chain and iced-out watch he has on, I can tell that he's really ballin'.

"Damn, girl, you still got a fat ass on you," Damien says as he grabs my ass.

"Let's just do this." I can't believe I'm about to sleep with this grimy-ass nigga. His every touch makes me sick.

"Oh, we gonna do this, ma, but first I want you to dance for me."

He's got to be kidding me. "I don't have any music."

"Just think of a song in your head and bounce that ass for me." Damien sits on the bed and takes his gun and puts it on the dresser on the other side of the bed. There's no chance of me grabbing it at all.

I start to slowly grind for him. Damien leans back on the bed and opens his legs. I slowly dance and unzip my jeans, pulling them down and over my ass to step out of them. I have on a pair of pink panties, and Damien palms my ass as I dance for him.

I try to make myself numb to stop thinking about him. He rubs his fingers over the sheer fabric of my panties and caresses my clit. You would think I'd be getting wet, but I only feel like throwing up.

His hands travel under my shirt and grab my titties. He then pulls my shirt over my head and sits me down in his lap as I continue to gyrate my waist to an imaginary song in my head. I can feel his hardness in his pants as he plays with my titties.

This is it. I might as well do this and get it over with. I don't want to look at his face while we do it, so I bend forward to click off the lamp. As I reach for the lamp, I notice that the base is made out of metal. I have one chance and I take it. I click off the lamp and then quickly grab it, swinging it around and busting Damien in the head.

Crack!

"Aarragh! What the fuck?" he yells in pain.

I keep on bashing him in the skull with the metal base, and blood splatters against the headboard. Damien tries to reach for his gun, but I don't give him a chance to get it. I deal him blow after blow to the skull, until he doesn't move, and I stand there shaking, not knowing if I've killed him or not. I drop the lamp and stand there frozen.

Then I see his chest move, and I swiftly grab the gun. I don't know what to do. I quickly put my clothes back on, and then I pick up my phone to call the police. Then it hits me. Instead of calling the police, I call Nikki.

I'm scared to death and tell her that Damien has taken me to a hotel and that I've beaten the shit outta him with a lamp.

Nikki is stunned, but then she gets Dre, and they quickly drive over to the hotel and find me in the room with Damien. His head is busted open and covered in blood.

"Oh God, Mo'Nique . . ." She hugs me.

"I was so scared. He said if I didn't go with him, he'd find you. . . ."

"It's okay. It's over now," Nikki tells me.

"Where's his gun?" Dre asks.

"Here." I give it to him.

Then this fucker Damien comes around. "Oh, shit. Look who it is. If it ain't my favorite bitch," he says.

Dre punches the shit outta him. "Watch your mouth, nigga."

Damien spits blood outta his mouth. "So, this is it, huh? You just gonna kill me?" Then Damien starts to laugh.

"What's so funny?" Nikki asks him.

"You, bitch. You weren't nothing but some good head. You and your bitch-ass cousin. Fuck y'all."

Nikki walks up to him on the bed and gets in his face. "You ain't shit, Damien. I wasn't nothing but good head, huh? Well, you know every time you kissed me, guess whose dick I had been sucking on?"

Damien glares at her.

"That's right, nigga. My dick," Dre says to him.

"All that shit you and Horse did to me didn't kill me. It just made me stronger." Nikki spits in his face.

"Bitch!" Damien yells.

"Nikki, take Mo'Nique and go to the car," Dre says.

Nikki and me walk out of the room and get in the car.

"Are you okay, Mo?"

"I'm fine."

"I'm so proud of you. You fought back." She hugs me again.

Nikki starts the car, and suddenly we hear a loud crack.Dre walks out of the hotel room, and we drive off down the road.

That night, I turn on the TV and see Fox 5 News reporting about a notorious drug dealer found dead in a Days Inn hotel room. Damien Ruffin had ties to hip-hop recording artist Kane. The police have no suspects and believe it was a drug deal gone wrong.

Dre tossed the gun in the river. Maybe this is wrong, but I feel good knowing that Dre was the one that killed him, considering what Damien had done to his cousin Rodney. Finally, after so much pain, this chapter in my life and Nikki's has been closed.

Epilogue

A Woman's Worth

JANELLE

I graduate from the University of Georgia today, and Jayson, Nikki, and Dre are there to cheer me on. After all the craziness in my life, this has got to be one of the most fulfilling things to ever happen to me.

When Jayson came back into town from L.A. a month ago, I told him everything that happened with Damien. I really didn't know how he would react to it, because he's still a cop. Jayson just asked me if there was anything left in the room that could be linked to me, and I told him Dre got rid of the lamp and the gun.

Jayson just caressed my face and told me that I did what I had to do, and that was the last we spoke of it. I guess Jayson just figured that sometimes you gotta go outside of the law in order to get justice done.

It's funny seeing Dre, an ex-drug dealer, and Jayson, an ex-undercover cop, sitting next to each other clapping their hands for me, but I guess life is filled with surprises.

After the ceremony, Jayson is driving us back to our place in Decatur.

"I never would've done this without you, Jayson."

"You don't give yourself enough credit. You're smart and beautiful. It was just going to be a matter of time before you realized what you were capable of," Jayson tells me.

"That might be true, but because of you I realized that a hell of a lot sooner."

We pull up to the house and walk in, and I see four suitcases packed and in the living room. "Jayson, what's going on?" I ask, confused.

"Oh, didn't I tell you? I bought tickets for us to go to Montego Bay, Jamaica. Happy graduation, baby."

"Oh my God! I love you, I love you, I love you!" I scream as I jump into his arms.

About two and a half hours later, we're on a flight to Jamaica. I've never been out of the country before. From what little I've heard about Jamaica, I know that it's a beautiful island.

When we get to Montego Bay I see what all the fuss is about. The water is brilliantly clear near the shores, and the cool island breeze feels so good.

Jayson arranged this whole trip months ago. I can't believe he did this for me.

After we check into our beachfront hotel, we find a club that's playing Buju Banton's "Champion Remix." I'm wearing a tight red-and-black summer dress. I move my waist to the music when "Time to have Sex" comes on, and I give Jayson a dirty grind on the floor. For once I don't mind flexing my stripper skills in public. From the rock in Jayson's pants, I can tell that he doesn't mind either.

"I love you, Janelle," Jayson says as he gazes into my eyes.

"I love you too. I've loved you from the first night we met," I tell him.

"I promise you that I'll never let anyone hurt you again," Jayson says.

"I know. And I'll never let anybody hurt you again either." Jayson kisses my lips tenderly.

That night we go back to the hotel about three in the morning, and it's on. I don't know if it's the margaritas or the island vibe, but Jayson and I make love to each other like we're in heat—up against the wall, on the couch, and then eventually on the bed. When we wake up in the morning, we have more hot sex.

All in all, this is the best vacation I've ever had. I never thought I'd be somewhere like here with a man I'm so in love with. I just feel like I haven't been living my life, and now I can truly begin.

***

NIKKI

Dre has been here with me for six months, and I can't believe that he's kept his word to me. He really has given up the game. It's not easy to walk away from it when that's all you know, especially when you're an ex-con and nobody wants to give you a job, but Dre's a hustler. He and a friend opened a little music store in midtown Atlanta that also makes custom grills. They call the place A-Town Grillz. Dre still has a little money put away that he refused to touch until now, so he could start this business.

I even quit my job and started to work there as a cashier. I'm more or less eye-candy for the guys that come in.

So much has changed in our lives, and still there's one more surprise.

That night, Dre comes home from the store, I cook him dinner, and we sit on the couch to watch TV.

"Dre, do you love me?"

"Yeah, I do. What kind of question is that?" Dre asks me.

"I just wanna make sure you're happy with me. I know there's a lot of other women around that you could be with."

"But none of them I've been in love with. Nikki, I done been with a lot of women, and none of them make me feel the way you do. I told you a long time ago you're the only lady I wanna be with. So why do you doubt me now?"

"I don't know. I guess because things change after a while. People change."

"That's true, but I haven't."

"Dre, I got something to tell you," I say nervously.

"What is it, Nikki?"

"I didn't think it could happen again after what happen to me, but . . ."

"But what? What's wrong?" Dre asks, concerned.

I look into his eyes and hope I'm doing the right thing. "I'm pregnant."

Dre doesn't say anything right away. He looks at me and then puts his plate on the coffee table. "Are you sure?"

"Yeah . . . I'm two weeks late, so I took a pregnancy test this morning. Shit, I took three different ones to make sure. Listen, Dre, I know you're just starting this business up, and I don't want you to feel like I'm trying to trap you into—"

Dre puts his finger over my lips. "Stop talking. I'm trying to think of a name for my little boy." Dre smiles at me. I feel like a world of pressure has just been lifted off my shoulders.

"Who says it's going to be a boy? It could be a girl."

"Naw, trust me, it's gonna be a boy." Dre puts his hands on my stomach and rubs my belly. "Junior."

"Oh, hell no. I'm not calling my boy Junior."

"See, you said *my boy*."

"That's not what I meant! Oh God, you're so aggravating," I say to him.

"And you're having my baby," Dre says and hugs me.

Is this really happening to me? I'm gonna have a baby. Dre is gonna be my baby daddy. After all the shit I used to talk about not wanting to get knocked up by no trick, this happens. Mo'Nique and Penny are gonna flip when they hear this.

Dre starts to make plans for us to buy a house in the next few months and makes sure I go see the doctor regularly. I can't believe this is the same man I used to think was too young and immature to handle a relationship. I guess I should have been looking in the mirror when I said that. This is the best thing that could ever happen to me.

JAYSON

Doing what's legal and getting justice can often be two different things. Too often in life, things are not black or white. There are areas of gray. After Janelle told me what Damien tried to do to her again, I was glad Dre killed him. As a cop, it's my job to arrest people like Dre, but as far as I'm concerned, he did the world a favor. Does that mean I'm a corrupt cop like Denzel in *Training Day*? No. It just means I'd rather see a murderer and rapist like Damien get what he deserves.

As for Vanessa, she was sentenced to twenty years in federal prison. Her lawyer was able to get some time knocked off because they took an early plea by the D.A. She was almost as bad as Damien. I guess with the divorce from Lauren, being undercover and seeing her again after so long, it clouded my judgment, but with all that chaos going on in my life, I still found Janelle.

Taking her to Jamaica for a week was something I wanted to do for a long time now. It's just amazing to me how much she has stood by my side throughout everything. I just hope I'm making the right decision by doing this now.

I've taken Janelle to a little Jamaican restaurant on the beach, and we sit at a table, eating some curried goat, white rice, and fried plantains.

"So, how does it taste?" I ask her.

"It's good! You know, when you told me it was goat meat, I didn't think I would like it, but it tastes so good!

"I told you it would be good." *Damn, she is so beautiful.*

"Janelle, you know, these past two years have been crazy. Even from the beginning when you thought I was Tommy Holloway you've been here for me."

"I told you, Jayson, it doesn't matter what your name is. I love you."

"Well, I'm glad you said that, because I wanna change your name now."

Janelle looks at me oddly, as if she knows what I'm going to do.

"Janelle, now that our lives are back to normal, I don't wanna spend the rest of my life without you," I say to her.

"Oh my God . . . Jayson?"

I take out a little blue ring box and open it and show her a fourteen-karat yellow gold diamond ring.

"So I'm asking you, Janelle Mo'Nique Taylor, will you please marry me?" I've never been this anxious in my life. Five years of undercover work and nothing has shocked me like this before.

Tears start to roll down her eyes. It's like she can't speak. "Yes . . . yes, I will."

I slide the ring on her finger.

"I love you, Janelle."

She gets up from the table and we share a passionate kiss.

"I love you too, Jayson."

This time I'm not going to screw up this marriage. This is really the beginning of our lives together.